Year of the Black Pony

Year of
the Black Pony

BY WALT MOREY

E. P. Dutton & Co., Inc.   New York

Library of Congress Cataloging in Publication Data

Morey, Walter   Year of the black pony

SUMMARY: A boy growing up in the Oregon country in
the early 1900's experiences the death of his father, the
remarriage of his mother, and the ultimate attainment of a
dream.

[1. Frontier and pioneer life—Fiction.   2. Family
life—Fiction.   3. Horses—Fiction] I. Title.
PZ7.M816Ye [Fic] 75-33805 ISBN 0-525-43455-0

Published simultaneously in Canada by Clarke, Irwin &
Company Limited, Toronto and Vancouver

Designed by Meri Shardin
Printed in the U.S.A.   First Edition
10 9 8 7 6 5 4 3 2 1

To F. Clarke Berryman, D.V.M.,
                whose help is appreciated

And to Don McRae,
                my neighbor who knows horses

I WAS LATE. I took off from the house running fast as I could. I rounded the barn, crossed the pasture, and started up the long slope that led to the top of Christmas Ridge. I ran until my throat was dry and my heart felt like it was about to jump out of my rib cage. Then the slope turned steep. I quit running and climbed the rest of the way.

The spine of Christmas Ridge is about fifty feet wide. It stretches for miles splitting the valley almost down the middle. There's an odd nest of big rocks up there about thirty feet high. I climbed to the topmost one and stretched out on my stomach. The valley rolled away beneath me, a spring-green carpet of new grass speckled with clumps of trees and brush. In the middle stood our typical homesteader's board-and-bat cabin, the two outbuildings, and the pattern of fences and gates.

My breathing gradually settled back to normal and my heart stopped pounding. I kept listening and looking. There was nothing. I was too late. I was about to get up and leave when I heard it. A faint rumble rode the morning silence like the roll of distant thunder. It swelled in volume. I got to my knees in excitement. My heart was hammering again.

They burst around a shoulder of the ridge a hundred yards away—fifteen or twenty horses running hard. They were Sam Fletcher's young stock that he let run loose on the open range. They followed the ridge every morning to feed in some distant part of the valley. At night a hired hand rode out and drove them home.

I had eyes for only one. The black pony in the lead. He ran like he loved being free. His head was up, sharp ears forward, black mane and tail flying in the wind. The sun made his black coat glisten like satin. The big muscles across shoulders and legs rippled like light flashes on water. They pounded past right under the rock where I crouched. I watched until they were out of sight. The whole thing took maybe two minutes.

Every Saturday since the winter weather had broken I'd climbed up here to watch that pony pass. The sight of him did something to me I've never quite been able to explain. He was more than tremendous strength and speed and beauty of motion. He set me dreaming. Thinking of him running so free, so eager, so full of the love of life, I could lose myself and forget for a time some of the bickering and quarreling that went on at home.

It hadn't been that way before we moved from Michigan two years ago. But this past year things changed. It was particularly bad last night. Ellie had one of her numerous bouts of sore throat and was asleep. I pretended to be but I heard every angry word Pa uttered. He had a nasty temper and for the first time I was afraid he might do Ma bodily harm.

I couldn't blame Pa altogether for the trouble at home. And certainly it wasn't Ma's fault. Somebody had to be strong. It took stiff-necked courage and grit to ranch in the Oregon country in the early 1900's. Pa used to say she had a ramrod up her back. "You don't give an inch. You get stiff-necked about it, brace your feet, and refuse to budge," he often said angrily.

Pa had no experience farming or ranching. He'd worked in a sawmill for years. But he always hated it. "I'm sick of getting up, of carrying a lunch bucket, going to work, coming home. I'm sick of living by a whistle." He wanted to get away, do something on his own. But sawmilling was all he knew.

Then a friend told him about ranching in the Oregon country. "Great place," he said. "Land's dirt cheap and grass is belly deep to a cow. Raise beef cattle. Nothin' to it, Harry. Let 'em run on the open range the year round. Maybe feed 'em a little wild grass hay a couple months in the winter. The rest of the year you just sit back in your rockin' chair and watch their bellies swell into money." The friend knew of three hundred acres for sale. There was a house on the place and a couple of outbuildings. "All ready to go to work," he'd said. "A widow wants to sell. It can be bought cheap."

Pa said happily, "That's for me, Mabel. No more lunch bucket. No more livin' by a whistle. I wanta take a day off, I'll take it. I'm gonna do somethin' for myself."

Ma had been raised on a farm. "It won't be that easy,"

she said. "It's a hard life with lots of work and long hours. You don't know anything about ranching."

"So I'll learn. If other men can do it, I can too. I'm workin' long hours now."

Apparently Ma believed him. Here we were, Ma, Pa, Ellie, and me about five miles from the little town of Sunrise. We had three hundred acres of land, nine head of cattle, a milk cow, one horse, a dozen chickens, and a board-and-bat cabin. It was all paid for out of our small savings. It was a terrible mistake.

That first year Pa learned he didn't take to ranch life. He had no interest in the land, crops, or animals and he had no intention of learning. He missed the monthly paycheck he'd got since he was sixteen. Here he earned much needed money only when he sold something, which wasn't often, or when he worked for some of the other settlers. He was handy with tools and did quite a bit of that.

Pa was not a good self-starter. All his life he'd either been told what to do or had to keep up with a machine. Ma knew what needed to be done on a ranch but Pa didn't take kindly to a woman telling him. He missed the smell of sawdust and the sound of a saw slicing through a log. And he especially missed the gossip and companionship of old sawmill friends with whom he used to stop at a bar on the way home nights, have a drink, and hash over happenings at the mill. Here he had only Ma, Ellie, and me. That is, until he got to going to town about once a week.

Pa had met the Graysons, half brothers, Arlo and Oliver. They owned a hardscrabble hill outfit a few miles out of town. Nothing grew on it but sagebrush and jack rabbits. Most of their time was spent in town, in the Pastime, when they had money. Nobody thought much of them but Pa. Even a twelve-year-old boy like me could see that sitting and drinking and swapping yarns with them was a little like being back home in Michigan talking and laughing with Pa's mill friends.

That wouldn't have been so bad but Arlo and Oliver got pretty wild when drinking, and Pa, with his quick temper and the aggravation of being stuck out here where he didn't like it, got quarrelsome. The Sheriff ordered the three of them out of town when they started a fight in the Pastime one day and broke up a table. After that Ma went to town with Pa whenever she could, to sort of ride herd on him.

It was getting warm on the rock. The spring sun was swinging straight overhead. I climbed down and headed home. I didn't want any trouble with Pa. He walloped me for being late getting home, or for not milking on time, or letting the woodbox get empty. If he knew I'd been sneaking up the ridge just to see a horse he'd tan me good.

When I rounded the barn Nellie was hitched to the buggy in front of the house and Ma and Pa were standing beside it talking. Pa was going to town but Ma didn't have on her coat and hat so she wasn't going with him. She must be staying home to nurse Ellie.

Pa scowled at me and said, "You been out galavantin' around the country again? Seems you're doin' a lot of that lately."

"I was just looking around," I said.

"What's to look at in this God-forsaken country? Sagebrush, jack rabbits, and boulders," he said bitterly and climbed into the buggy.

I didn't answer.

Ma said, "Now, remember, Harry, flour, salt, coffee." She ticked off on her fingers. "And don't forget Ellie's medicine and get back fast as you can. She needs it."

"Sure, sure." He scowled at me again. "You keep that woodbox full and pump some more water for the cattle and quit rammin' around the country." He picked up the reins and clucked to Nellie. They went out of the yard, the reins hanging halfway to the ground.

Ma started to call after him, "Harry, pick up the reins," as she had so often. Then she just shook her head and turned back into the house. Pa would never learn.

Time dragged. Noon came. The sun started swinging down the sky toward Christmas Ridge. I filled the woodbox and cut more wood, gathered the eggs and pumped the trough full of water for the cattle. Ma had Ellie gargle salt water and kept putting hot towels around her throat. She seemed to be feeling better. In between times Ma would step outside, shade her eyes, and stare up the valley looking for Pa. We both knew he'd met the Grayson brothers in town and was spending what money he had left with them in the Pastime. Ma's lips got tighter and tighter, her back straighter. I suspect she'd have ridden in after him if we'd had another horse, or even walked the five miles if she could have left Ellie. Ma was that kind of determined woman.

The sun started bouncing along the top of Christmas Ridge. I drove Fawn in and went to the house for the bucket to milk. Then I heard a horse and buggy come into the yard. We both ran to the door.

It was Sheriff Peck. He was in our buggy and driving Nellie. His saddle horse was tied behind. Pa wasn't with him.

6

I got an odd feeling in the pit of my stomach as I watched him get out of the buggy and walk to the porch where Ma and I waited. He said, "Mrs. Fellows, your husband has met with an accident."

Ma said, "I guessed as much when I saw you driving Nellie. Is he hurt bad?"

"Yes," he said, "very bad."

"He never would hold the reins up the way he should," Ma said. "Did the horse run away and throw him out?"

"No, ma'am, it wasn't like that at all. There was a fight."

"A fight?" Ma asked.

The Sheriff nodded. "With Frank Chase, out on the Creek Road. I don't have all the facts yet. But I will have. Way I heard it, it was an accident that got Harry."

"How bad is he hurt?"

"I wish there was another way to say this, ma'am." He shook his head. "Harry was hurt fatal. He's dead."

Ma just stood there for maybe half a minute and looked at the Sheriff. Then she said in the quietest voice I've ever heard her use, "You said a fight. But it was an accident. How can that be?"

"The fight was only part of it," the Sheriff said. "Harry drowned in the creek. It's pretty high this time of year with the spring run-off, you know. There'll be a hearing in Judge Beam's chambers in a couple of days to establish just what did happen. Not a trial, you understand, a hearing." His voice went on and on, giving Ma the few facts he had so far.

But I wan't listening. I was looking at Ma. Her dark head was up and her back had that ramrod-up-it look that Pa hated. Never before or since has she seemed so tall, so calm, so composed. But there was a terrible tenseness about her as if she held all the emotion and shock a human could stand in her two clenched fists and would not let it out. For myself that odd feeling kept growing and growing in my stomach until it was more than I could bear.

I ran back into the house and slammed the door.

THE HEARING was held right after Pa's funeral a couple of days later. It was the only excitement the town had known in months and the room was crowded. Ma, Ellie, and I sat in the front row. Ellie kept looking around. I don't think at seven she knew what was going on.

Judge Beam heard Frank Chase first.

I'd seen Mr. Chase a number of times in town. He lived in a board-and-bat cabin on a side road a couple of miles beyond us. He had about thirty head of cattle and raised some alfalfa. Everybody said he was a good rancher and that if anybody made it homesteading he would.

I looked at him now and thought, this is the man that killed Pa. I expected him to look different somehow. He was tall and rawboned. He looked rawhide tough. His shoulders stretched taut his old wrinkled blue coat and his hands were wide and thick. His hair was jet black and heavy brows gave him a perpetual scowling look. There was a sizable lump on one cheek, several long scratches, a skinned spot on his chin, and his mouth was swollen out of shape.

He gave his name, though everybody knew him, and promised to tell the truth.

Then the Judge said, "Now, Mr. Chase, in your own words, just what happened?"

"I was coming back from the Hamiltons' where I'd delivered a load of hay," he said in a low voice. "The front wheel hit a rock and broke. The axle hit the ground and tilted the wagon bed. It startled the horses and before I could stop them they'd pulled the wagon crossways of the road, blocking it. The road's real narrow there," he explained. "There's a steep bank on one side. The other drops almost sheer to the creek about twenty feet below. The creek's deep and swift at that spot. I was trying to work a pole under the axle to lift it out of the dirt so the team could pull it when these fellows came along."

"What fellows?" Judge Beam asked.

"Why, Arlo and Oliver Grayson and Harry Fellows, Your Honor."

"Go on," the Judge said.

"Harry Fellows seemed to be in a big hurry and he couldn't get past. I tried to explain that I'd have the road clear in a few minutes. But he wouldn't listen. He began yelling and swearing. I guess Arlo and Oliver Grayson thought it was a great joke. They kept hollering and laughing and urging him on. Next thing I knew Harry jumped outa the buggy and began beating my team with his whip. I took the whip away and threw it in the creek."

"Then what happened?"

"He came at me with his fists, fightin' mad. I didn't want to hit him, him being drunk and all. So I kept backing away and telling him to cut it out. But he just kept coming and throwing punches at me. He hit me some pretty hard ones."

"What were the Graysons doing all this time?"

"Sitting on their horses cheering him on. I guess it was a good show to them."

"Did they try to stop him at any time?"

Chase shook his head. "They didn't even get off their horses until it was all over."

"Did Harry Fellows put those marks on your face?"

"He sure did. The more I tried to talk to him the madder he seemed to get. I finally realized there was only one way out and I hit him as hard as I could."

"Where did you hit him? And with what?"

"On the point of the chin, with this." Chase held up his big right fist. "If he'd been sober it'd probably knocked him down and that'd been the last of it."

"What did happen?"

"He went down all right. Then he sort of rolled around like a sack of loose grain. Maybe he was trying to get up. I don't know. Anyway, he went over the edge of the bank and rolled right into the creek. It's deep there and fast. He yelled once that he couldn't swim, then he sank. I ran down the road almost a hundred yards to where I could get to the water and where it's shallow. I waded out waist deep and pretty soon here he came tumbling over and over about a foot under water. I hauled him out and carried him ashore."

"What were the Graysons doing all this time?"

"I don't know. I wasn't paying any attention. But they weren't helping me."

"Go on."

"That's about all, Your Honor. The Sheriff came down the bank a minute later and we tried to revive Harry. But it wasn't any use."

Sheriff Peck spoke next.

He looked big and sure and confident. He explained that he'd gone into the Pastime that fateful afternoon and found Pa and the Graysons there and had ordered them out of town. "They'd done quite a bit of damage in there a few months before when they went on a spree. I could see trouble comin' again."

"How could you see it coming, Sheriff?"

"They were getting loud and quarrelsome with other customers. Harry Fellows had challenged a man to a fight but others pulled them apart. I like to nip trouble in the bud. I thought I'd done that when I told the three of them to go home."

"Then what happened, Sheriff?"

"They all left town together. Fellows was in the buggy, Arlo and Oliver were on horseback. I followed behind them a few minutes later. I was going out to Mel Hansen's to see about a missing horse and I came on the scene with the broken wagon just like Frank Chase described it."

"What were the Graysons doing?"

"As I remember when I got there, they were just sitting on their horses staring down the road at Frank Chase like they couldn't believe what happened."

The Judge next called Arlo Grayson. Arlo was short and stocky. His blond hair was too long and his gray eyes were so pale they seemed to have no color. There was a look of sloppy flabbiness about him. Everybody knew he was Oliver's shadow. Whatever Oliver did Arlo followed suit. That day he was pretty subdued. He chewed his lower lip and kept glancing at his brother. With the Sheriff sitting there he didn't dare deny anything. Little by little Judge Beam wormed out all that the Sheriff and Frank Chase had testified to. He kept mumbling, "Well, yes. Sorta. It was like that, I guess." Then he'd glance at the Sheriff and mutter, "Yes, sir, that's how it was."

It was not that easy with Oliver. He was a husky, brawling man who'd been in scrapes of one kind or another ever since we'd come to Sunrise. He wasn't intimidated by Judge Beam or the Sheriff. "Sure," he admitted, his voice loud and confident, "the Sheriff told us to leave town. But we wasn't causin' no trouble. The Sheriff got a little excited, that's all. So we left. We'd had our fun anyhow."

When the Judge asked how Fellows reacted to the wagon and team blocking the road Oliver said, "Harry asked 'im real civil like to move the wagon so's he could get past with the buggy. When Chase said he couldn't, Harry got out to show 'im how. Chase got mad when Harry hit the horses with a buggy whip to start 'em. You know that kinda whip only stings a little."

"Tell me about the fight," Judge Beam said.

Oliver shrugged. "Just a little old fight. Wasn't much."

"The lumps on Mr. Chase's face seem to indicate that Mr. Fellows took it pretty seriously," the Judge said.

Oliver turned and scowled deliberately at Frank Chase. "Them little lumps and scratches ain't nothin'," he said. "I've beat up men worse'n that and had a drink with 'em the next day. Anyhow, there wasn't no call to hit Harry that hard with him drunk and all."

"You admit he was drunk?"

"Drunk, sure. But not fallin' down drunk, Judge. Just drunk enough so's he couldn't fight worth a lick and couldn't stand up after bein' hit so hard. Chase shoulda hit 'im just hard enough to stop 'im, not knock 'im down the bank into the creek where he drowned."

"How hard would you hit a man just to stop him?" Judge Beam asked.

"Can't rightly say just how hard." Oliver squared his shoulders and added, "But I could sure demonstrate it, Your Honor."

Judge Beam just looked at Oliver. He didn't ask any more questions.

The hearing was over a few minutes later. Judge Beam summed it up. "There's no question Harry Fellows precipitated the fight that brought on his death. Mr. Chase does have a certain moral responsibility for having struck him so hard. On the other hand, a man has the right to defend himself. This is simply a tragic accident that could easily have been avoided."

We were outside and had got into the buggy when Frank Chase came up to us. "Missus Fellows," he said awkwardly, "I can't tell you how sorry I am. If I'd even dreamed anything like this might happen I'd have let Harry beat on me all day or I'd have run away. If there's anything I can do to help you and your children I hope you'll let me know."

"Thank you, Mr. Chase," said Ma formally.

"What will you do now?" he asked.

Ma's head came up and her shoulders squared. "Why," she said, "we'll go right on living where we are. We'll manage." She slapped Nellie with the reins and we drove off.

14

At home I unharnessed Nellie, turned her into the pasture, then went into the house. Ma set Ellie and me down at the table, then put her hands flat on its top and said in a crisp, business-like voice, "Now, then, it's all over. We've done our crying. We're not going around moaning and complaining about our hard lot. We've got to think about living and to do that, we've got to be very practical about this. The good Lord helps those who help themselves, and we've got a lot of helping ourselves to do." As Pa would have said, Ma had her feet braced. She was meeting adversity head on. She wasn't giving an inch.

Ellie wiped her nose and eyes and just looked at Ma. She didn't look too good yet. She wasn't quite over her bout with sore throat and she'd done a lot of crying.

"We've all got to do our share to keep this household running," Ma continued. "Ellie, your job will be to do dishes night and morning, set the table, clear it away. See that the floor is kept swept and clean, the beds made every morning. And keep up your schoolwork without Mother having to continually remind you. Do you understand?"

Ellie nodded. She began to cry again.

"Christopher," Ma said to me, "you're the man of the family now. You've got to do the chores you did before, plus Dad's work and keep up your school grades, too. Of course I'll help you both every way I can. We're going to take each day as it comes and do the best we can. I'm sure everything will turn out all right."

Ellie started crying hard and Ma put her arms around her to comfort her.

I went out back of the barn to do my crying. It was the last time I cried over Pa's death.

Spring was here. It was time to put in a garden, and

this year we'd need an especially big one what with so little money to buy things. We had no team or plow so I spaded it by hand nights and on weekends. I dragged it smooth with one section of harrow behind Nellie. Then I planted it to peas, carrots, radishes, cabbage, and a lot of corn and potatoes. Our soil was rich and with the warm spring weather the rows were soon showing. I spent countless hours hoeing. It seemed to me we were going to spend all spring, summer, and fall accumulating food and stuff that we'd spend all winter getting rid of.

The woodpile had gone down alarmingly during the winter. Now I had to cut for the summer and fall as well as for the coming winter. That meant a lot of wood. There was a boggy spot about a quarter mile from the house where Pa had cut wood before. It held scrub pine, willow, juniper, and several other good fire kinds. We had a two-man, six-foot-long crosscut saw. I could handle it alone bucking up a tree into stovewood lengths, once I had a tree on the ground. But I needed help felling it. Ma would come down and help me fell a couple, then leave me to do the rest alone. Ma was a slender woman, not built along the husky lines of many farm women. Pulling a crosscut saw was mighty hard for her and we had to stop to rest many times. I worked there every weekend, sawing, splitting, and hauling wood to the house with Nellie hitched to a one-horse cart Pa had made.

I often thought of the black pony running Christmas Ridge. But I never went up to see him again. There was too much work to do. I fell into bed every night bone tired. My school grades suffered a little. Ellie's didn't. But then she always was a better student than I was.

Those first weeks some members of the congregation

drove out several times to see how we were making out. Ma would see them coming, rush to put on a fresh apron, and pat her shining black hair into place. She'd meet them at the door with a smile and cheerful words and invite them in. Grief, Ma insisted, was a private thing. You didn't burden your friends with it. They'd sit and drink tea and eat cookies Ma had made and ask how we were managing.

"We're getting along fine," Ma would say. "Much better than I expected."

"You look a little thin, Mabel, a little drawn, maybe," Mrs. Adams observed.

"You do look a little peaked," Mrs. Wood said. "I'll bet you're working too hard, maybe worryin', too."

Ma smiled. "Well, you know I never was the draft horse type. I've always been more on race horse lines."

Reverend Jackson drove out twice. He was young, slight, and intense. The weight of his first parish bore heavily on his thin shoulders. "Some of the ladies think you look a bit tired and worn," he said. "I'm afraid I agree. Are you sure you're all right? Everything is going well?"

"Reverend," Ma said, "I won't say we're having it easy, because we're not. But we are getting along. We're working and we're staying together. To me that's the most important of all."

"Yes," he agreed. "Of course." On leaving he said, "If there's anything I can do to help I expect you to let me know. That's the main reason I'm here."

"I shall certainly come to you," Ma said.

Later I took a good look at Ma. Maybe she was a bit thinner but to me she looked healthy enough.

For a time it did seem we were getting along all right. But gradually I began to realize, and I know Ma did, too, that no matter how hard we worked there was trouble ahead. We could raise plenty of hay for our milk cow, Fawn, for Nellie, and the nine head of beef to take them through the coming winter. But how could I harvest it? The first cutting of alfalfa would be ready in a few weeks and I needed a mowing machine and hay rake. Pa had traded carpenter work to Sam Fletcher for the use of those tools. So I rode to Fletcher's bareback on Nellie one Saturday.

Sam Fletcher was a small man with a shock of gray hair hidden under a big floppy hat and a wide friendly grin. He had lived in the valley a long time and was the most successful rancher around. "Son," he squinted at me, "you got the muscle and know-how to put a heavy roof on a shed?"

"No, sir," I said.

"That's what your Dad traded for the use of tools. And that's what I need."

I thought of the black pony and small band of young stock that ran free and said, "Maybe I could take those horses out in the morning and bring them back at night. That'd save you a man."

He shook his head. "You a good rider? You got a good horse?"

"I've got Nellie," I said.

He looked at Nellie standing half asleep. "Why that band would run your old mare to death the first morning. Anyway we just open the gate and they take off on their own in the morning. I send a man to drive 'em in at night. By then I can spare a hand. Tell you what, when I get through this fall, if there's time, I'll come help you out.

I've got a thousand head of stock to care for. That comes first and we're mighty busy now. Of course if you'd like to sell those nine head of yours I'll take 'em off your Ma's hands for—say—twenty dollars a head."

I thanked him, got on Nellie, and rode off.

I began to realize that while Pa complained a lot he'd also done quite a bit of work around the valley, too. His working out not only got the loan of tools but brought in badly needed cash money as well. Cash money we had to have for clothing and food we couldn't raise, like flour, salt, beans, and such. Cash money was all important.

While Ellie and I were in school during the day Ma went to town in the buggy and tried to find work. She asked at the hotel and both restaurants. There was nothing. She heard the livery stable wanted a boy. But they wanted one that could be there seven days a week. She considered opening a dress shop and sewing for the local women. A woman was already doing that and wasn't very busy.

The whole problem was that most of these homesteaders were as poor as we were and some were even more ignorant of ranching. They were Eastern bank clerks, factory workers, schoolteachers. They'd come out here with the same dream Pa had. To get away from the drudgery of a job and work for themselves. They arrived with nothing or very little. If they hung on for five years they got title to the land. The little cash money they had went for some kind of house, an outbuilding or two, a minimum of stock and machinery, and the barest staples. Whatever hiring they did was to put up buildings. That's where Pa got the cash money we needed to live. But those homesteaders had no work for a twelve-year-old boy.

I woke up one night and Ma was sitting at the table

frowning at a paper covered with figures. I went and sat beside her. She looked tired. She'd helped me fell a tree that day.

She indicated the page of figures and said, "I've been trying to make twenty dollars do the work of a hundred. And you know, that arithmetic hasn't been invented yet."

I didn't want to think about leaving but I had to ask, "Would selling the cattle and Nellie bring us enough to take us back East or to some big city?"

"It'd take us, but it wouldn't keep us until I could find something to do. There aren't many jobs for women, you know." She looked at the figures thoughtfully. "We're in a rather unique position. I've no folks to go to. Your father had a brother but he never approved of me so he certainly wouldn't help us. Anything done we'll have to do on our own."

"How much money do we have?" I asked.

"About twenty dollars. But with spring and the garden coming on, and the canned stuff left over from winter we can get through the summer all right."

"What about next winter and when the money's gone?"

"That's the sticker. We can't let it come to that. The practical thing is to plan now so we never reach that spot." She was quiet a moment, then said, "The ideal solution would be to leave somehow."

"How can we with no money?"

"I don't know yet. I'm working on that."

And she was. I often heard her padding quietly about the house when she thought Ellie and I were asleep. And night after night I watched through half-closed lids as she sat at the table reading her Bible.

One night about a week after our first talk she came out

after supper and helped me hoe in the garden until dark. We sat on the steps later to rest before going in. Ellie had done the dishes, finished her homework, and had gone to bed. The stars were out bright and there was a full moon. Our land rolled away under the soft light right up to the foot of Christmas Ridge that rose ragged and stark against the night sky.

There was no breeze. It was utterly still.

Ma sat with her chin in her hands staring into the night. "I sit in there at the table and try to think things through and my mind keeps going around like a squirrel in a cage," she said. "I come out here and look at this and everything seems to straighten itself out."

"You figured what we're going to do?" I asked.

She nodded. "I haven't worked out all the details yet."

"Will we have to leave?"

"Yes. We can't possibly stay here this winter."

"How soon will we leave?"

"Very soon now."

"I'll hate to leave."

"So will I." She rose and looked down at me soberly. "One thing I can tell you. We're going to stay together." Then she went into the house.

Saturday morning I was getting ready to milk when Ma said, "When you finish milking put a halter on Fawn and tie her to the back of the buggy. Then hitch up Nellie and bring the buggy around. We'll all change into our best clothes. We're leaving here."

My heart dropped right out of my chest. "You mean now? This morning?"

Ma gave me a straight look. "This morning, Christopher."

"What about the cattle? What about the chickens? We can't leave them."

"Only for a little while," Ma said. "They'll be taken care of."

Ellie asked, "You mean, get all dressed up like going to church?"

"That's right, honey. Like going to church."

"Where we going?" I asked.

"Christopher," her voice was sharper than I've ever heard it, "I have it all worked out. You'll learn soon enough." When Ma's voice got that edge and she had that head-up, back-straight, lips-pressed-together look, you quit asking questions.

An hour later we were ready. Ma had on her best black dress, black gloves, hat, and shawl. She also had Pa's old valise that I stowed behind the seat.

We went up the valley, Ma driving, Ellie on one side, me on the other, and Fawn plodding patiently behind. None of us talked.

After a couple of miles we turned up a lane and Ma pulled up at a cabin.

I said, "But, Ma . . ."

She said in that same sharp voice, "Christopher, bring the valise. Ellie, get out."

We marched up to the cabin and Ma rapped sharply. After a minute the door opened and Frank Chase said, surprised, "Why, Mrs. Fellows!"

"May we come in?" Ma asked.

"Of course." He stepped back and the three of us marched in. I put the heavy valise down at my feet.

"This is a surprise." Mr. Chase was obviously flustered. He had about a week's growth of beard and his black hair stood on end. He combed fingers hastily through his hair and said, "I've been meaning to get over to see you. But I've been real busy, and to tell the truth the time just sort of gets away from a man."

"I know," Ma said. "It's spring. That's when us farmers really have to work." She drew a deep breath and said, "Mr. Chase, the day of the hearing in town you said that if ever there was anything you could do to help me and the children to let you know."

"That I did," Chase said.

Ma's dark head was high. Her gray eyes looked straight into his brown ones. "Mr. Chase," she said coolly, "whether Harry Fellows was at fault or not in that fight you two had is not the problem. He provided a roof over our heads, put clothing on our backs, and food in our stomachs. You took that away from us. That's why we're here. Now you can take care of us."

Frank Chase looked at Ma, then at me, then at Ellie, then down at the valise, then at Ma again. He acted like he hadn't heard right, or couldn't believe what he'd heard. He scrubbed a big hand across his face and through his hair again and finally said, "Well, now, Missus Fellows, it wasn't necessary for all of you to come. You could have sent your boy and I'd have come right over."

"That wouldn't have been enough," Ma said.

He glanced at the valise again. "I don't understand."

"It's really quite simple," Ma said. "We can no longer go on living on our place without a man. We can grow things, we can even eat—up to a point. But it takes a certain amount of cash money to live there. Harry furnished that. Now, without him, we haven't any. Also, there are some kinds of work on a ranch a boy can't do."

Mr. Chase nodded. "It does take a man to do some things. As for the money part, we're all caught in that bind."

"So here we are," Ma said.

"So I see," he said. I knew he didn't. Neither did I, but I was beginning to get an inkling and I figured he was too, the way he kept stealing glances at the valise.

"You want me to keep your cow while you go someplace, is that it?" he asked.

"I want you to keep the cow," Ma said. "And us."

He couldn't have been more surprised if Ma'd hit him in the head with a club. He started to smile, polite, then he didn't. He scowled at Ma, then at me, then at Ellie. "Whoa!" he said, "back up. Let's get this straight. You mean here? In this house? All three of you?"

"All three of us," Ma said. "In this house."

"Well, for the love of Mike!" he exploded. "Look around. You see any place to stay? I live in this one room."

"I know." Ma sat down calmly on one of the benches. Ellie and I ranged ourselves on either side of her.

"Then you're sure not what I thought you were. You propose to live here—with me—in this house." He was almost shouting. The big veins stood out in his neck. His face was red. He pointed a big finger at Ma. "Listen to me. I always respected you as a fine upstanding lady of high moral character. I admired you, from a distance, of course. Now you breeze in here with a bald-faced proposition like this." He shook his head in disbelief. "Of some others in this valley I'd have believed this possible. Of you, no!"

Ma's chin shot up. Her back straightened. "Mr. Chase,

you have jumped to a completely wrong conclusion."

"Do you know what'd happen if we did that? The good people of Sunrise would ride both of us outa this valley on a rail. And they should."

"No they wouldn't," Ma said quietly. "Reverend Jackson can take care of that."

"Reverend Jackson!" Again he looked like Ma had belted him with a club. "So, that's it!"

He jumped up so quickly the bench fell over with a crash. Tall, lean, glaring menacingly from beneath scowling brows, he looked like a man who could knock another down a twenty-foot bank with a single punch. A small fear sprang up in me. He leaned across the table and shook a finger under Ma's nose. "You're figuring to sneak up on my blind side. Well, let me tell you something. I don't have one."

"Of course you don't," Ma said.

"Just so you understand. You're not trapping me into anything like that. Oh, no. No, sir. Not by all that's holy you don't. No siree, Bob. If I'd wanted a wife I'd of got one myself long ago. But I don't want one. I don't need one."

"You need one all right." Ma was calm as could be. "Look at you, out at the knees and elbows. Overalls and shirt none too clean either, and not pressed. You're a sight."

"I suit me fine."

"And look at this place," Ma went on as if she hadn't heard. "Practically no food on these shelves. And such shelves, boards nailed to the wall. No curtains to hide the food or anything. No curtains on the windows. Why, I'll bet you live on pancakes, biscuits, meat, and potatoes. I could save you money."

"With two kids?" he said quickly.

"With two children, one milk cow, a horse and good buggy, nine head of beef in good condition, and a dozen laying hens that we can move over here. That is worth considering, Mr. Chase."

"You tellin' me four can live cheaper than one?"

"Not cheaper, better. That shirt and those pants will be in tatters soon. You'll have to buy new. I'd patch them so neat you'd hardly know it and all it'd cost would be a spool of thread. And you'd eat right for a change. Have a few cooked vegetables, a variety."

"Don't care much for vegetables."

"You've probably never eaten them."

"I'm healthy as a horse," Chase insisted. "Never had a sick day in my life."

"You will," Ma said. "Can't abuse the inner man without the outer one eventually paying for it."

"I'll pay and be glad. What're you trying to do, throw me off the track? We was talkin' about you wantin' to get married."

"Not wanting," Ma corrected him, "needing to."

"You need to. I don't. I don't want to hear any more of that kind of talk. How'd you get started thinking on that line anyhow?"

"If you'll sit down, be a little calm and listen, I'll explain. Then you can decide for yourself if it's a logical and practical solution for all of us."

"Don't include me in that logical, practical stuff," Mr. Chase said.

Ma stood up and walked about the big room. She was nibbling thoughtfully at the tip of a finger, a habit she had when she was deep in thought. "Our house might be a little bigger, not much. We made three rooms of it. Two for bedrooms and one to live and cook in. The same can be done here. A partition could go right across there, just behind the stove. That would make one bedroom. A door could be cut in that far wall, a lean-to roof and side walls added to make another bedroom. That way you'd have your bedroom at one end of the house, the children and I at the other."

"Wait a minute," Mr. Chase said annoyed. "One minute you talk about going to Reverend Jackson. The next you're splittin' the house down the middle and adding extra rooms. You're not making much sense."

"I'm making nothing but sense," Ma said. "This will be a marriage in name only. A convenience for both of us. I'm not looking for a husband any more than you are a wife. But I know no other way to keep the children and me together."

"I understand that. Don't get me wrong," he said hastily. "This marriage of convenience thing, and you having your part of the house and me mine sounds a lot better than I thought you was gonna say. But you talk about adding rooms and changing things like there was all the time in the world to do it. Where do you figure that time's comin' from?"

"I estimate it will be at least another three weeks before the first cutting of alfalfa is ready. You and Christopher can sleep in the barn during that time," Ma said. "I've heard you built this cabin, so you're handy with tools, as Harry was. Harry would do this job in about three or four weeks."

"I suppose you've figured out the rest of it, too."

"I think so. We can move our furniture over here. That will give us plenty. Christopher's cut a lot of wood.

That'll save the time of cutting any. We can move the chickens and cattle right away. The cattle can be turned in with yours and the chickens can roost in the barn till Christopher and you build a lean-to for them."

"You've thought of everything," Mr. Chase said.

"I've tried to. And I might add, that of those nine head of cattle, six will be calving late this summer. That's as good as saying we're bringing over fifteen head."

"If they all live," Chase said dryly.

"You'll see that they do."

"Thanks for the confidence. You got anything else?"

"Christopher has a dandy garden started. He can harvest that and you'll be eating fresh vegetables for a change. You'll also be getting three hot meals a day, your clothes mended, washed, and ironed, fresh milk twice a day, butter, cream, and eggs and your house kept spick and span and looking like a home."

"I get all that for taking on three more people and having my house torn up and enlarged," Chase said dryly. "I can do without it."

"In a month or two you'll wonder how you got along without us," Ma said.

"With all this scheming of yours, you've left out the most important part. Maybe Reverend Jackson won't go for this."

"I think he will."

"Figured that out, too?"

"There's nothing to figure. I just think that when he understands the situation he'll perform the ceremony. He must recognize that we live in a rough, new land where sometimes it's necessary to do unorthodox things."

"So you've got faith," he said. "Well, I haven't."

"When that's all you have left to go on," Ma said quietly, "that's what you use. From the very beginning I was banking that you were the kind of man who meant what he said that day in town."

Frank Chase didn't say anything for the longest time but I could see that he was doing a powerful lot of thinking. Those black brows were pulled down until they almost hid his brown eyes. He kept kneading one big fist into the palm of the other hand. Finally he sort of sighed and stood up. "Guess I should have known a thing like this couldn't end with just a court hearing. If I only hadn't taken that one single punch at Harry. But I did. There's no getting around that."

He sort of pulled back his big shoulders and straightened his back. "I'll probably wish a thousand times I'd never said this. But—all right, I'll go along with your idea. We'll give it a big try, but you'll have to talk Reverend Jackson into it. Don't expect any help from me. I tell you right now, lady, my heart's not in this. Not one little bit."

Ma said quietly, "Neither is mine, Mr. Chase. Believe me! Neither is mine."

I'LL BET ours was the oddest-looking wedding party the valley's ever seen.

We drove in to Sunrise in the buggy. Ma, Mr. Chase, and Ellie sat in the seat. I sat in the box behind and let my legs dangle. Mr. Chase drove. His long length was hunched over, elbows on knees. He held the reins lightly and looked straight ahead. He had shaved, put on the wrinkled blue suit that he'd worn at the hearing, and he wore a tie. Ma sat on the far side of the seat, very erect, head high, looking straight ahead. Ellie sat between them. Ma and Mr. Chase didn't exchange two words all the way to town. Ellie chattered for a little while but no one paid any attention and she finally stopped. I don't think she understood what was going on. I did, and I didn't like having this big grim-looking man taking Pa's place. The thought of being with him every day kept a small fear alive.

Mr. Chase let Nellie poke along at a slow walk as if he was postponing the inevitable to the last possible moment.

We stopped at the courthouse and Ma and Mr. Chase went in and got the license. Then we drove on through town to Reverend Jackson's.

The church was at the far end of town on a slight rise of ground. The Reverend and his wife lived in a small parsonage behind the church.

Reverend Jackson answered Ma's knock. He smiled and said, "Why, Mrs. Fellows—and Mr. Chase! Come in. Come in. Georgia!" he called into the kitchen, "we have company."

Mrs. Jackson was as thin as her husband. She had big solemn gray eyes and brown hair piled high on her head. It made her look taller than the Reverend.

They sat down in straight-backed chairs facing each other, all except Ellie and me. We stood on either side of Ma. The Reverend and his wife looked at us and we looked back at them. They seemed at a loss for words, probably because they were so startled to see Ma and Mr. Chase together.

Mr. Chase was as uncomfortable as a grasshopper in a hot skillet. He didn't seem to know what to do with his big hands. He pulled at the fingers of his right hand until I expected to hear the knuckles crack. Realizing what he was doing, he folded his arms across his chest. Then he held his hands, fingers laced tightly together, between his knees. Finally he put a hand on each knee, straightened his arms and sort of braced himself as if he expected to get hit an awful wallop.

Ma seemed the only calm, comfortable person there. She sat straight and tall and smiled at Reverend Jackson and his wife.

Reverend Jackson finally spoke to Mr. Chase like he was trying to put him at ease. "I haven't seen you at services the past few weeks."

Mr. Chase shook his head. "There's an awful lot of work on a ranch with spring and all."

"I can imagine. But man should labor six days and rest on the seventh."

"Kind of hard to explain that to cattle and a growing crop," Mr. Chase said.

"I know," Reverend Jackson said. "And how do the cattle and crops seem?"

"Little early to tell about the alfalfa but it looks like a good first cutting. If we don't get a rain to spoil it. Cattle came through the winter fine."

Reverend Jackson then turned to Ma. "And how are things out your way, Mrs. Fellows?"

"With the cattle, chickens, and alfalfa, they're fine," Ma said. "With us they aren't good."

"When I was out there not long ago you said everything was going well."

"That was my hope, Reverend. But we're licked. The children and I simply can't go on living there. That's why we've come to you."

"What can I do to help?"

"Mr. Chase and I have talked it over and we've arrived at a decision—that the best interests of all can be served only by us getting married."

"Married! You two?" Reverend Jackson adjusted his glasses. His big blue eyes turned from Ma to Mr. Chase. "That's why you're here? You want me to perform a marriage?"

"That's correct," Ma said.

Mr. Chase nodded.

"I see. I see." Reverend Jackson rubbed his thin hands together. I guess he'd never bargained on meeting this kind of problem. He was suddenly nervous, I almost might say embarrassed. "Don't you think, that under the circumstances, you're—well—rushing things a bit? It would appear much better if you waited say six months, or even a year."

"It would probably look better," Ma agreed. She explained about the shortage of money and that there were things needed doing on a ranch that only a man could do.

Reverend Jackson frowned thoughtfully. "I understand. But in view of the unfortunate tragedy, and the fact that you will be married a long time, I still think it wise to make every effort to wait."

"If we do," Ma pointed out, "the children and I must have help to live at our place. That means that Mr. Chase will be coming over quite often for one reason or another. He hasn't the time to take care of two places, and the very fact that he'd come would start tongues wagging. Believe me, Reverend, I know how gossip can run wild in a small town. This is the only practical way, and facing up to it openly will stop talk."

"That's possible," Jackson agreed. "I wasn't thinking of gossip altogether. There's another consideration that should be more important to both of you. Gossip would eventually die out."

"What could that be?"

"Neither of you has said one word about love and affection."

"Reverend," Ma said, "I've read the Bible from cover to cover many times. And it's full of things about widows remarrying and wives good to their husbands and families. But I've found little about love and affection between husband and wife. It often refers to respect and goodness and it does state that the price of a good wife is far above rubies. I intend to be a good wife."

Reverend Jackson looked at Mr. Chase. "Do you agree with Mrs. Fellow's statements?"

Mr. Chase nodded. "I sure do. Yes, sir, I do."

"Of course, you understand, I can't perform this ceremony without a license."

Mr. Chase took the license from his pocket and extended it without a word.

Reverend Jackson looked at it. "Everything seems to be in order."

"Reverend," Ma asked, "is there any legal reason we shouldn't marry?"

"No, no legal reason."

"We came to you because this is the only church in town and you are our pastor. But if you'd rather not perform this ceremony we'll go back to Judge Beam."

"That won't be necessary. I was only trying to point out what I consider valid reasons for waiting. But since you're both determined I'll perform the ceremony."

There was only one small hitch. When the Reverend asked for the ring Mr. Chase looked blank. But Ma calmly slipped her wedding band off and handed it to him.

After the short ceremony, Reverend Jackson and his wife shook hands with Ma and Mr. Chase and wished them well. Reverend Jackson said, "I hope what we've done is the right thing and that everything works out as you want it to. If there is ever something I can do to help, please let me know."

Ma said, "It was the only practical solution, Reverend. Now we'll simply have to work at it."

"Yes," he agreed, "you will."

I sat in back again as we drove through town and out the road leading to Frank Chase's cabin. Again Mr. Chase was hunched over, elbows on knees, holding the reins loosely in his hands, letting Nellie take her own sweet time. Something of the seriousness of the occasion got through to Ellie and for once she was quiet. Ma sat as she had before, very erect, her head high, looking straight ahead. The only sounds I remember were the soft plop of Nellie's feet in the dust and the wheels running over an occasional rock.

Mr. Chase spoke only once all the way back. "Lucky you had a ring. I never even thought about one. Only thing I could have given you would have been a bent horseshoe nail."

"It doesn't matter," Ma said.

At the cabin Ma got dinner from the lean stores of food on Mr. Chase's shelves. But Chase said afterward it was the best meal he'd eaten in a long time.

"It will be better," Ma said, "when we get our food over here."

There was still a good part of the afternoon left. Ma and Mr. Chase decided that he and I should take the wagon and go to our old place to bring back our food, bedclothes, and the chickens.

While he went to hitch up Ma talked to Ellie and me. She set us down at the table and said, "Now, then, I want you both to remember that my name is now Mrs. Mabel Chase, not Fellows any more," she said for Ellie's benefit. "We changed that at the minister's this morning."

"Is our name Chase now, too?" I asked.

"No, you are still Christopher Fellows and Ellie Fellows."

Ellie puckered up ready to cry. "You're not our mother any more?"

"Of course I am, honey. But now that we're going to live with Mr. Chase in his house I have his name, that's all. Mr. Chase is known as your stepfather. He'll take care of us just as Daddy used to. Now do you understand?"

"I guess so," Ellie sniffed.

Ma put an arm around her and said, "It's going to be all right. Mother says so. Now," she looked straight at me, "you're both to obey Mr. Chase just as if he was your real father. I don't want to hear of you arguing or sassing him. If he tells you to do something, do it. Christopher, is that clear?"

I nodded. But she kept talking straight at me. "I'm sure you'll find Mr. Chase a fair and just man. If things do go wrong and it seems like there may be trouble you're to come to me. If you're right I'll stand up for you just as I did with your father. If you aren't I won't. Do you understand?"

I said, "Yes."

"Another thing. You may have to give a little," Ma warned. "Always remember we're intruding on his way of living. This isn't easy for him, taking on a family. Being a bachelor he may not have been around children much. He's got to get used to us as we've got to get used to him. We're all strangers. It's going to take a little time to get to know each other."

"All right," I said. I thought of something and asked, "Ma, what do we call him?"

"Mr. Chase, of course," Ma said promptly.

A minute later the wagon rattled around to the front of the house.

Mr. Chase had a good wagon and a fast-stepping team named Jess and Gyp. We got to our place in less than half an hour. By the time we loaded all our food and stripped the beds of blankets, sheets, and pillows the sun was dropping and night was seeping into the sky. We waited about half an hour. Then the chickens went to roost. It was no problem catching them and stuffing them into gunny sacks.

Ma and Ellie had supper ready when we got back. By the time we'd eaten, unloaded the wagon, turned the chickens loose in the barn, and I'd milked Fawn it was getting late.

The hay in the barn made mighty soft sleeping. We each had two blankets. I spread one on the hay. The other I rolled up in. Mr. Chase spread his blanket a few feet away. We didn't talk. In fact, all the time we'd worked together at our place we'd hardly said a word. I was a little afraid of him.

He sat up a long time and stared out the open barn door at the night like a big lean black shadow. He might have been stone except I heard him sigh and mutter under his breath, "What a day. Lord, what a day!"

It was very still. The chickens complained sleepily. Nellie wandered past the door. Beyond Mr. Chase I could see a square of night sky and the stars. I kept thinking, that man over there is my stepfather.

Ma's name is Mrs. Mabel Chase. It didn't sound right. That man had taken Pa's place. His home was now our home. I had to work with him every day. He had the right to whale the daylights out of me just like Pa used to. I wondered what kind of temper he had. Pretty bad, I decided. The thought of him laying a hand on me turned me cold.

I thought of Reverend Jackson's last words as we left his house. "I hope what we've done is the right thing and that everything works out as you want it to."

I just didn't see how it could.

SUNDAY MORNING we held a conference on whether to go to church or not. To me it didn't matter. Ellie wanted to go. That was exciting to her, seeing the other people, listening to the singing, and above all getting dressed up. She kept yelling, "I want to go," until Ma told her to be quiet.

Mr. Chase said, "I'm against it. If we walk in there together, everybody's going to know."

"They're going to know in a few days anyway," Ma said. "What better way for the whole valley to find out than for us to go in there this morning like a family?"

"I don't like it," Mr. Chase said. "People talking, whispering behind their hands, staring at us."

"I don't think they will," Ma said, "not if we go to church together. If we walk in there acting perfectly natural they'll wonder a little, of course. We've got to expect that."

"I haven't been attending as regular as I should," Mr. Chase hedged. "When you've got work to do you let it slip."

"Most ranchers do, especially in the spring. Reverend Jackson and everybody in the valley understands that."

Ellie opened her mouth again but Ma stopped her with a look.

"All right," Mr. Chase finally said, "if you think you can pull it off."

"We'll pull it off," Ma said.

We went in the buggy, just as we had yesterday. Mr. Chase drove. This time he sat straight and held the lines up snug. Ma had pressed his suit and shirt. He looked as neat as any man. Nellie sensed a difference and trotted along at a smart clip.

We were late and services were about to begin. The small church was almost full. Mr. Chase started to slip into an almost empty pew in back, but Ma marched right down the aisle about two-thirds the way to the front where there was a vacant pew. We all followed. There'd been a faint buzz of talk as there always was before services began. I noticed as we went forward it sort of fell off. By the time we sat down you could have heard a pin drop—almost. After a minute the low talk began again and went on about as usual until the Reverend stepped to the pulpit.

Mr. Chase's ears were red and he looked down at his hands. Ma sat through the service erect and prim, looking straight at Reverend Jackson, paying close attention to every word. Not once did she glance right or left. She held Ellie's hand and when Ellie wanted to gawk around Ma gave it a warning squeeze. I stole a couple of looks, and I could see we got a few quick glances, especially from the women. But there was no whispering behind hands. It seemed to me like the usual Sunday service.

At the end we walked out with the rest of the congregation and Reverend Jackson made a point of speaking to Ma and Mr. Chase. Some of the men spoke to Mr. Chase and women nodded and smiled at Ma. We got in the buggy and drove off.

Mr. Chase wiped his face with a handkerchief and said, "Longest sermon I ever sat through."

"It was the usual length," Ma said, "an hour."

"Seemed like at least two to me. But you brought it off," he said admiringly. "I didn't think it could be done, but you brought that whole bunch to heel."

"There wasn't a woman or man there that didn't know that what we did was the only practical thing," Ma said. "Reverend Jackson helped, too."

"Sure, he helped," Mr. Chase agreed. "But it was you who had this figured right down to a gnat's eye."

After lunch Mr. Chase hitched Jess and Gyp to the wagon to go to our old place for a load of furniture and anything else Ma thought we might need. She and Ellie went in the wagon. I rode Nellie bareback so I could drive our cattle back to Mr. Chase's.

While they loaded up the wagon I rounded up the cattle. As I drove them to the house Mr. Chase came out. "They look good," he said. "Nice and fat. Why don't you go on? Take plenty of time, don't let 'em run. We'll be along as soon as we get loaded."

I was about halfway when they passed me. Ellie waved and yelled. This was all fun for her.

We now had about a mile farther to go to school so we rode Nellie, me in front, Ellie behind, her arms around my waist to hold on. We had our books strapped together and we carried lunches in small blue lard pails.

Ma saw us off. She gave me a meaningful look and said, "You take care of Ellie."

I kind of figured at school something might happen, like a kid saying something nasty, but nobody did. Bill Lyons sort of grinned and said, "I seen you in church yesterday."

I doubled up my fists and walked right up to him. If anybody started talk or poking fun at us it'd be him. I was about as big as he was. I looked him right in the eye and said, "Sure. I saw you, too. What about it?"

He shrugged. "Nothin'. I seen you, that's all." He knew I was ready for him.

Ma was a great organizer and Mr. Chase was a fast worker with saw and hammer. Within a week they had practically transformed the inside of that cabin so you'd hardly know it. In a couple of days Mr. Chase had built a partition across one end of the room making a bedroom for Ma and Ellie. They moved our big bed in there. My cot went against the other side of the partition. Mr. Chase's single bunk went into an opposite corner of the room where they hung a blanket to give him privacy. Next he punched a hole through the wall for a door and built on a lean-to for his bedroom.

Ma hung the curtains from our old place on the windows and put the braided rug on the floor near the table. She made flour-sack curtains and hung them across the open food shelves to hide pots and pans and food boxes.

Mr. Chase looked at it and confessed, "Sure looks better'n it did. Not a bachelor's quarters any more."

"Curtains at the windows, rug on the floor, fire in the stove, the smell of cooking and you've got a home," Ma said proudly.

43

"Got to admit I get much more of this kind of cooking I'll gain twenty pounds."

"You need twenty pounds on that big frame."

"Then I'll be fat. And a fat rancher is a lazy rancher," Mr. Chase said.

When school was out three weeks later we were all settled in and things were running smooth. Ellie had a last small bout with sore throat. Then Ma figured she was through with that until winter set in again.

But changes did take place, some that I'd never have suspected. For one, Ellie got along fine with Mr. Chase right off. In no time she was tagging him about chattering away.

A couple of times Ma said, "Ellie!" pretty sharp. She tried to divert Ellie's attention to something like setting the table or gathering the eggs, one of her chores.

One night while Mr. Chase was reading the little weekly paper she crawled up in his lap like she used to with Pa.

Ma said sharply, "Ellie! don't bother Mr. Chase."

"She's not bothering me," he said quietly, "she's bothering you. There's no need to include the kids in this formal set-up you've devised."

Ma's lips got tight and her head came up as it always did but she didn't say anything, and Ellie stayed. I heard Ma say to him once later, "You do seem to have a way with children."

"I should," he answered, "I was the oldest of four boys and two girls."

Ma had worked out a kind of formal set-up all right. She'd practically split the house down the middle right at the stove. She moved the table over that imaginary line so that his end was on his side. The easy chair with the cow-hide bottom was there, too. And over there were his lean-to bedroom, his clothes, the deer-horn rack that held his rifle and shotgun. Maybe he just naturally gravitated to that side of the room because his things were there. Anyway, he spent very little time on our side of the house.

Ma called him Mr. Chase except when they were around other people, like at church, or when Reverend Jackson and several of the ladies came to call. Then she said Frank.

In some ways he adjusted better than Ma. He had a sly kind of humor that delighted in sticking pins in her. Ellie started calling him Daddy Frank and when Ma said sharply, "Ellie! I've told you. . . ." Mr. Chase interrupted with, "What's wrong? Are you afraid of losing her?"

"Certainly not," Ma said.

"You must be. Seems to me a mother should be mighty pleased if her child came to like her stepfather."

"You should understand," Ma said stiffly.

"I don't. Why don't you spell it out for me good and plain."

Ma couldn't, or wouldn't, and Ellie kept calling him Daddy Frank.

He called Ma Mabel all the time and she finally reminded him coolly that it wasn't necessary at home.

"Seems to me that's where it's most necessary," he said. "But, then, I'm not a very good hypocrite."

"Meaning I am?"

"Not at all," he smiled. "We were talking about me." I'm sure he enjoyed ruffling her feathers. But Ma didn't give an inch.

45

For myself I got along with him, but I was careful. I called him Mr. Chase. He called me Boy. Whenever I worked with him I did whatever he asked as well as possible. But he made no friendly advances, and I certainly didn't. I couldn't accept him the way Ellie did. That small fear of him which sprang up in me the first morning never left. I couldn't help wondering what he'd do to me if he really lost his temper. What if he started beating me the way Pa used to?

With school out I began riding Nellie over to our old place every other day. I watered and hoed the garden and carried back a sack of vegetables each trip. In between times I worked with Mr. Chase. We built a small shed for the chickens. Then I helped grease the rake and mower, get the hay rack on, and turned the grindstone for hours while he sharpened the sickle bar in preparation for mowing.

Mr. Chase cut his fifteen acres one day. The next day he went to our old place and cut the ten. He let both fields lie until the hay was dry then hitched Jess and Gyp to the big rake and let me do the raking. I had no trouble except that my windrows were crooked. But Mr. Chase said it didn't matter. He followed behind with a pitchfork and built the windrows into shocks.

He let me handle the team on the hay wagon when we hauled it in. He pitched the shocks onto the wagon where I spread them and built the load. I wasn't very good at it but he didn't seem to mind. It took two days to haul in his fifteen acres. The next day he spent in the barn moving the hay around to make room for more. I took the team and rake to our old place to windrow the ten acres he'd cut.

46

It was three days since I'd been there and the garden was beginning to suffer. I spent about two hours pumping and carrying water to it. The sun was standing right overhead when I finally headed into the alfalfa field.

I had to rake especially slow because Pa hadn't done a good job leveling the land before seeding it. The teeth bounced at even a slow walk and I missed some. It was mighty monotonous.

The sun was about halfway down the western sky when for the first time in weeks I began thinking of Fletcher's black pony. I kept thinking about him as I made round after round. There were about a dozen rounds left when I knew I had to see him again. I glanced at the lowering sun. It was about time for the hired hand to ride out and drive them in. They could be thundering along the ridge any time now. I could slip up there, watch them pass, and get back to finish the raking in plenty of time.

I lifted the rake and drove as far up the slope as I dared. I tied the team to a stump at the edge of a brush patch and began hiking toward the top.

It didn't take more than twenty minutes to reach the rock pile where I always watched. I stretched out on my stomach to wait. About half a mile down I could see the patch of brush where the team was tied but I couldn't see them. Beyond was the green square of the alfalfa field with my pattern of windrows.

Time passed. The sun sank lower. The band of horses didn't come. I stood up on the rock to look, but it didn't help. I couldn't wait much longer. It would take at least another hour to finish the raking. Maybe Fletcher wasn't letting them run loose any more, or maybe they'd already gone by. The sun was dropping toward the top of a single

47

big pine tree far in the distance. When it hit the top, I told myself, I'd have to leave.

The sun hit the top of the tree. I realized then that climbing up here to see a half-wild pony was a silly kid trick. What difference could it make whether I ever saw him again or not? He was Fletcher's horse. It was time I quit dreaming an impossible dream. I stood up to leave and that moment I heard the familiar distant thunder of pounding hoofs. I froze. My heart climbed into my throat as it always did at the thought of seeing him again.

Here they came, bursting up onto the ridge in a boil of dust and tossing manes and heads. The black pony was in the lead. He ran as he always did, head high, mane and tail snapping. His nostrils were spread wide until I could see the rim of red, running on the wings of the wind, like he loved being free. They pounded past under me. One of Fletcher's riders brought up the rear.

I watched until they rounded the shoulder of rock and were gone. It took a couple of minutes for the excitement in me to die down. Then I went racing down the steep slope to the brush patch where I'd tied the team.

They were gone.

I just stood there and looked at the stump with the broken rein still wrapped around it. I couldn't believe it. I glanced around expecting to see them standing near eating alfalfa. They were nowhere in sight. Something had spooked them. They'd broken the rein and taken off. I'd seen a runaway once and terrified horses are a scary sight. Anything could happen. And in this big, open country they could be anywhere, maybe miles away by now.

I began searching the ground for tracks or something to indicate the direction they'd gone. I saw where windrows had been scattered. Walking horses wouldn't do that. They'd have stopped to eat. Farther on windrows were broken apart. That seemed to head them in the direction of the barn and house. I tore out fast as I could run.

When I rounded the corner of the barn there they stood in the barnyard quietly waiting for someone to let them in. The rake was still hitched to them, but the first thing I saw was one iron wheel badly bent.

I walked around the team, patted them and talked quietly as I inspected the harness. They appeared to have been here some time. They weren't sweaty, and they were no longer nervous as runaways would normally be. Several harness straps were broken letting the gear sag to one side. One rein was still intact. Tugs, collars, hames were all right.

Next I inspected the rake carefully and I began to feel sick. One side of the iron wheel was dented in at least six inches. Five spokes were bent. Three rake teeth were almost straight. A half-dozen others were bent at varying angles. This rake could not be used. I doubted it could be repaired.

Mr. Chase would have to buy a new rake, and maybe he didn't have the money. Without a rake two more cuttings of alfalfa would go to waste in the field. There'd be no feed to carry the cattle through the winter. The loss of this rake could break Mr. Chase.

I picked up a rock and began trying to hammer the dent out of the wheel. It did no good, but I had to do something. Tears started and I couldn't stop them. I wiped them away and kept hammering.

Then Frank Chase's voice said behind me, "What happened? You have a runaway?"

He was riding Nellie bareback. He slid off and dropped the reins. "When you didn't come home I figured something must have happened." He walked around the team inspecting the harness, talking half to himself. "I can fix this. I've got extra strap and rivets. No special problems here." He came back to the rake.

I said, "It's ruined. It's ruined. And it's all my fault!" I began hammering the wheel again. The tears kept coming.

He took the rock from me and said, "Suppose we look it all over before we make any rash decisions." He began a careful inspection of the rake. "I can straighten most of these teeth myself. Three of 'em will have to go to the blacksmith shop along with the wheel."

"The rake's not ruined? It can be fixed?" I asked.

"Of course it can be fixed. This's bad, but I've seen worse. It'll hold us up a couple of days, but luckily there's no rain in sight so we won't lose any of this hay by it getting wet. What happened anyway? Something spook the team? Say something, Boy."

I'd have known exactly what to expect from Pa. He'd have started yelling like mad and then I'd have got it. Good. No questions, no explanations asked for. Mr. Chase had me completely confused. He was calm, quiet.

For just an instant I thought of manufacturing some kind of lie. But I knew immediately it wouldn't work. This man had more knowledge of horses, ranching, and machinery than I did.

"I don't know what happened," I said.

"What do you mean you don't know?"

"I—I wasn't with them when they ran away."

"You weren't on the rake? Well, maybe you were lucky. You could have been hurt bad."

"I wasn't anywhere near," I said miserably. "I tied the

team to a stump and climbed to the top of Christmas Ridge."

He put his big fists on his hips and stared at me. "That's just a barren ridge. What were you doin' up there?"

I wiped my nose with my sleeve. Here it came, I thought, a crazy explanation that was no excuse at all. "I—I went up there to see a horse."

"A horse?" He just looked at me for maybe half a minute. Then he leaned against the side of the rake, folded his arms and said, "Tell me about it."

I told him about Fletcher's young stock and how I'd been watching them all spring. He listened without saying a word. "Going up there was a crazy thing to do," I finished.

"Didn't seem like it at the time, did it?"

I shook my head. "Only after I came down and found the team gone."

"I've seen that band of young stuff," he said. "Which one catches your eye?"

I wondered if he was playing with me like a cat a mouse before he began beating me half to death as I deserved. "A black pony," I said.

He nodded. "I know the one. Full of life and fire. You've got a good eye for horseflesh. But that animal's no good for anything."

"I don't understand," I said.

"He could have made a fine horse. But he's been ruined. He's an outlaw. Starts to buck the minute a rider hits the saddle. Fletcher keeps him to have fun with around the Fourth of July or any other gatherings of people. He's been ridden, I hear, but he always puts up a terrific fight. Animal like that's no good on a ranch."

"What made him an outlaw?" I was saying anything to

try to hold his interest, to put off the beating I was sure I was going to get. I kept watching for those brown eyes to turn almost black and the heavy brows to come down in the ugly scowl that meant he was angry.

"He's been abused by men," Frank Chase said. "Now there's a pony you can walk up to if you're careful, put a halter on, and even lead. But the minute your leg goes over his back he starts to fight. He figures he has to."

Dreaming about such a horse made this runaway seem even worse. No matter what Mr. Chase did to me he'd probably never trust me again with the team.

"Did you finish the raking?" he asked.

"I had about another hour."

"We'll come over in the morning, remove the wheel and damaged teeth and take 'em in to the blacksmith. When they're fixed you can come back and finish. Probably day after tomorrow."

"You'd trust me with the team after this?"

"Why not? You think you're the only person that ever pulled a dumb trick? I'd bet my bottom dollar it won't happen again. Besides, a boy should daydream a little. I did and so'd every kid I know." He smiled. "I had two big dreams. The horse I wanted was white as snow and belonged to the richest man in town. It was a sight to see him on that horse. I didn't have a chance in the world of ever owning that animal and I knew it. But that didn't stop me dreaming about it. I wanted him so bad it hurt."

"What was your other dream?" I asked.

"A thousand head of fat beef cattle roaming my own land. That, your Ma would say, was the practical one. I'm still working on it. To date, counting your Ma's stock, I'm about nine hundred and sixty-one head short."

I knew then there'd be no licking. I was relieved, and in a crazy kind of way a little disappointed, because now I was more confused than ever about Frank Chase.

"Guess we'd better be getting home so I can fix this harness yet tonight. You want to ride Nellie? You're lighter. I'll ride Jess."

We rode side by side, him in one road rut me in the other, Gyp following. I asked, "What could have spooked them?"

"No telling. A pheasant jumping out of the grass at their feet, a rabbit. I once had a runaway when a piece of paper blew up in front of the team. Maybe it was a good thing you weren't on the rake. You might not have been able to hold 'em."

We were almost home when he observed, "Your Ma's gonna wonder what happened."

"I know," I said.

"It's over and done. There's no sense bothering her with details. She know about you going to watch that black pony of Fletcher's run?"

"No."

"Good. Then let me handle the explanations." We rode along in silence. Then he said, half to himself, "Quite a woman, your Ma. Yes siree, Bob, quite a woman."

SURE ENOUGH, the first thing Ma asked when we rode in was, "What took so long?"

"A little runaway," Mr. Chase said easily. "Bent a wheel on the rake. We'll have to take it to the blacksmith to be straightened."

"Did you get thrown off or jump?" Ma asked me.

"Lucky for him he was off the rake when they spooked," Mr. Chase said. He nudged Jess in the ribs and went on to the barn.

I followed.

As we unharnessed and fed the horses I said, "It looks like she believed you."

"Why not?" he said. "I didn't lie. I just didn't tell quite all of it. But don't sell your Ma short. She's a smart woman."

Ma didn't ask any more questions but Ellie did. I'd like

to have wrung her neck. "Why'd they run away, Daddy Frank?"

Mr. Chase said, "Horses run away for a thousand reasons, Baby. And sometimes for no reason at all. But I'd guess a bee stung 'em. There's a lot of bees in the alfalfa this time of year."

That satisfied Ellie and no one spoke of it again.

After supper we mended the harnesses in the barn by lantern light. When we finally finished Mr. Chase proclaimed them as good as ever. The main trouble had been rivets that had pulled out.

Early next morning we left to repair the rake. Ma gave Mr. Chase a list of things she wanted from the store. At our old home place we removed the bent teeth and I held each one across a block while Mr. Chase hammered it into the proper shape again. It was almost noon when we finished, took off the bent wheel and the remaining bad teeth, and headed for town.

The blacksmith shop in Sunrise was one of the main social places for men to gather. There were always two or three lounging on the old buggy cushions placed for seats against the shop wall. The place smelled of smoke and horses and the hot blast of the forge. I loved to see the sparks fly, the flames leap and the iron turn cherry red, and then watch as Hank Manning bent and shaped it with mighty blows from one of a dozen or more big hammers.

There was only one old man sitting on a buggy seat that day. Spring and early summer were busy seasons. Ranchers had little time to sit and gossip when they came to town.

Hank Manning, bare-armed and bare-chested, was putting a new tongue in a wagon. He came out and looked at our bent wheel and teeth. "I can fix these easy," he said. "It'll be an hour or so before I can get to 'em. You in a big rush?"

"We've got part of a field left to rake."

"You're in a rush. I've got to get this tongue in a wagon first, and it don't wanta fit."

Mr. Chase said, "I'll help, if that'll speed things up."

"It sure will."

Frank Chase stripped off his coat and the two men went to work. I sat on one of the buggy seats to enjoy the smells and sounds and activity. They had the tongue bolted in place in less than an hour and pushed the wagon outside. Then they went to work on our wheel and the bent rake teeth. I wanted to stay and watch. But Mr. Chase handed me the grocery slip and said, "We can save some time if you'll go to the store and give this to Mr. Wright. I'll pick you up over there as soon as we finish."

I crossed the street to Wright's General Merchandise. Just before I entered I saw Arlo and Oliver Grayson going into the Pastime. It was the first time I'd seen them since the hearing on Pa's death.

I handed the list to Mr. Wright to fill out. He was an old man with snow-white hair. He always wore a spotlessly clean green apron that came to his knees.

I said, "If you can leave the stuff here on the counter Mr. Chase will pick it up when he comes from the blacksmith shop."

Mr. Wright nodded, adjusted his thick glasses, and squinted at the list, mumbling, "Flour, lamp chimney, salt, sugar, pepper, a gallon of coal oil. Fine, fine."

While I waited for Mr. Chase I wandered through the store looking at a whole world of merchandise. Besides groceries there were sections of bolts of cloth, shoes, hardware, harnesses, guns, clothing, and even toys. I'd never had much time to wander through here and look at all the things before. Today I enjoyed myself.

I finally came to the gun rack and there I stopped. A little single-shot .22 rifle caught my eye. It looked exactly like the big guns only smaller. Mr. Wright came by and asked, "See anything there you like?"

"That .22," I said.

"Nice little gun. For some reason it don't sell. Guess the young fellows now days all want repeaters. Silly. It only takes one shot to bring down game. No sense spraying the landscape with lead. Expensive, too."

"Yes, sir," I said.

A man and woman came in, bought an armload of groceries, and left. A woman brought in a little boy about two or three. Mr. Wright spent a lot of time fitting him with shoes. A couple of ladies wandered in, came to the bolts of cloth and began looking them over. I was still admiring the little .22 when Mr. Chase pulled up out front and came inside. I went to meet him.

Arlo and Oliver Grayson came through the door behind him. Mr. Chase went to the counter, looked over the stack of articles, and took out his purse. Mr. Wright left the two women and came to the grocery section.

Arlo leaned half smiling against a frame that held a great variety of handles. His colorless eyes watched Oliver. Oliver stopped a few feet behind Mr. Chase, spread his legs, and put his hands on his hips. The two weren't drunk, but they'd been drinking. I got a funny feeling in the pit of my stomach.

Oliver said, "Well! well! the big man comes to town,

Arlo. Ya' know who this is? This's the big, brave man that killed Harry Fellows."

"I know." Arlo kept smiling. "And Harry so drunk he could hardly stand up."

"You think maybe he could lick me, Arlo? I can stand up. See."

Mr. Chase glanced around and was aware of them for the first time. He turned back to Mr. Wright and counted out the money for our supplies.

Oliver went on talking. "You think maybe he can lick me, Arlo? A man as can stand on two legs and fight back?"

"Never in this world." Arlo grinned.

Mr. Chase tossed the sack of flour to his shoulder and said to me, "You bring the rest, Boy." He started toward the door.

Oliver blocked his path. Mr. Chase stopped and said very quietly, "All right, boys. You've had your fun."

"Not quite, we ain't," Oliver said.

Mr. Wright said in a frightened voice, "Now, boys. Now, now! I don't want any trouble in here. Take your quarrel outside."

I had stopped by a case of pocket knives too surprised and scared to move.

Arlo said to Mr. Wright, "Shut up, old man." He stepped to the counter, leaned forward, and slammed his fist into Mr. Wright's chest. The storekeeper stumbled back and fell against the shelves.

The two women who'd been edging toward the door bolted outside.

Oliver said to Mr. Chase, "You've had this comin' for months and now you're gonna get it." He hauled back his fist and hit Mr. Chase flush on the chin. Mr. Chase stumbled back, lost his hold on the flour and it fell to the floor. The sack burst open and flour spilled out. Then Oliver went after Mr. Chase swinging both fists. "This's for Harry," he shouted.

Frank Chase began backing away. He had both hands up warding off the flying fists. He didn't try to hit Oliver. He kept saying, "All right, Oliver. All right. Just cool down. Cool down. Don't be a fool, man. I'm not looking for trouble with you."

Mr. Wright came up from behind the counter, ran the length, and scuttled out the door. He raced up the street, his green apron flying.

Arlo began chanting, "Give it to 'im, Oliver. Sock 'im again. Show him how it is to fight a real man." Oliver landed a hard punch alongside Mr. Chase's head, staggering him. Arlo yelled gleefully, "That's a boy! That's showin' him. Bust him again."

Mr. Chase kept backing away trying to avoid the punches. He did avoid some, but many landed. Oliver hit him in the chin and staggered him again. A punch grazed his cheek drawing an angry red trail that began to ooze blood. And yet he hadn't punched back. He kept sliding away, still trying to talk to Oliver. He backed completely around the rack that held the handles and I could see he was heading toward the door to get outside. Oliver saw what he was doing, ran around the rack, and cut him off. He threw another wild punch. I guess Mr. Chase saw then that there was no use trying to reason further. That big right fist shot out and Oliver stopped as if he'd hit a wall. A second punch smashed him between the eyes and he fell over backward.

That's when Arlo took a hand. He ran in behind Mr. Chase, hit him on the back of the neck and knocked him down. Oliver jumped up and they both began kicking Mr. Chase. But for a big man he was surprisingly quick. He rolled out of the way of the flying feet and came up. Arlo grabbed him and pinned his arms to his sides. Oliver planted his feet and began smashing Mr. Chase in the face with both fists.

That was more than I could stand. Without even thinking I ran up behind Arlo, jumped on him and grabbed both hands full of long blond hair. I began to yank. His head snapped back and forth but I couldn't make him let go. His ear was right close to my mouth and the temptation was too great. I leaned forward, got a mouthful of ear, and clamped down hard as I could. Arlo squalled like a scalded cat. He tried to shake me loose but I had an awful good hold on his hair. Then he tried to twist his head and pull his ear out of my teeth. But I had a mighty good bite. He let go of Mr. Chase with one arm, punched back over his shoulder and hit me in the face. But I hung on. He hit me a second time, and a third. I lost my bite and fell off. He whirled and smashed me in the mouth. I sailed backward into the rack of handles, knocked the rack over, and sprawled among the handles.

Mr. Chase spun around, hit Arlo on the chin, then turned back to face Oliver.

Arlo stumbled backward, lost his balance, and fell beside me. He started to crawl out of the mess of rolling handles on all fours. I picked up the first handle handy. To this day I couldn't tell you what it was, but I brought it down on Arlo's head with both hands as hard as I could swing. The handle broke. But it sure took Arlo out of the fight. He went flat on his face and didn't move. I sat there holding the stub of handle. If he tried to get up I was going to whack him again.

I watched Mr. Chase wade into Oliver Grayson. Oliver could fight all right. He was about the same height as Mr. Chase but his fists weren't as big and hard, and his shoulders weren't as broad. Mr. Chase was mad. Those black brows were pulled down in an ugly scowl and I could barely see his eyes. In about a minute Oliver learned he was in bad trouble. He started backing away, trying to defend himself. I saw then what those big shoulders could do. Every time Mr. Chase hit Oliver he hurt him, and he was hitting him a lot.

Mr. Chase finally knocked Oliver sprawling and he tried to crawl toward the front door to get away. Mr. Chase grabbed his legs, hauled him back, lifted him to his feet, and knocked him down again. Oliver grabbed a handle. Mr. Chase jumped on the hand with his heel and ground it until Oliver yelled and dropped the handle. Then he yanked Oliver up again, held him at arm's length with one hand, deliberately cocked his right fist, measured Oliver, and swung. It sounded like a butcher dropping a side of beef on a meat block. Oliver folded up flat on his face.

Then Sheriff Peck came through the door followed by Mr. Wright.

Arlo was beginning to stir and groan. Sheriff Peck hauled him out of the mess of handles and propped him against the counter. He rolled Oliver over, slapped his face hard a couple of times, and dragged him to Arlo. He clamped handcuffs on both of them.

Mr. Chase lifted me up and asked, "You all right, Boy?" He got out a handkerchief and began wiping my mouth.

There was blood on the handkerchief. I tasted it in my mouth.

Mr. Chase was panting and there was blood on his face from half a dozen cuts and bruises. "I'm all right," I said. "How about you?"

"I think we'll both live," he smiled.

Sheriff Peck asked, "Son, how'd you get mixed up in this ruckus?"

"He came to my rescue," Mr. Chase said. "I was in real trouble when he took on Arlo."

"Kind of overmatched yourself, didn't you, Son?" the Sheriff asked.

"I guess so," I said.

"He might have been overmatched a little," Mr. Chase said, "but he took Arlo out of the fight permanently."

"Is that a fact?" The Sheriff looked me over. "You're quite a tiger."

Then we all just stood there and looked around. The grocery section of the store was a mess. Mr. Chase, Oliver, and Arlo had stomped through the spilled flour and scattered it over everything like dust. Handles were everywhere. The frame that held them was smashed flat. A gunny sack of peanuts had been spilled. A couple of cases of canned goods had broken open and peaches and tomato cans had rolled in all directions.

Mr. Chase shook his head. "I'm sorry, Mr. Wright."

Mr. Wright said, "Not your fault, Frank. You done your best to avoid this fight. I saw what happened. Nobody could have done more than you did."

"I'd been watchin' those two for a couple of hours," Sheriff Peck said, "just waitin' for the right time to move in and order 'em outa town. I could see trouble brewin'.

Guess I waited a little too long. They're gonna pay for this, Mr. Wright, right down to the last grain of flour."

Oliver and Arlo were beginning to stir and sit up. The Sheriff leaned over them and said, "You hear that, both of you? You're gonna pay for this whole mess, if you have to sell every cow on your place and the place, too. And you're going to jail on top of it. Then if I ever catch you in town again I'll toss you both in jail on sight." He hauled them to their feet and shoved them out the door. They looked pretty beat up. Arlo had a knot on his head big as an egg where the handle had cracked him and his ear kept dripping blood. Oliver's face was a mess. One eye was closing, his nose was knocked to one side and bleeding and his mouth was puffed like a balloon.

Mr. Wright got us another sack of flour. Then Mr. Chase and I helped him gather up all the handles, canned food, and peanuts and carried the broken handle rack outside. Then we took our own stuff, got into the wagon, and drove out of town.

My mouth was on fire. It kept bleeding and swelling. I discovered I also had a small gash alongside my right eye. It kept oozing blood. Mr. Chase dabbed at his own numerous cuts. Two buttons on his shirt were gone and his right sleeve was torn half off. I was surprised his face didn't look worse considering the many times Oliver hit him. I felt pretty shaky and I noticed that Mr. Chase kept drawing deep breaths.

We came to the creek about a mile out of town and Mr. Chase pulled off the road. "We'd better wash up a little before we get home," he said. "Your face don't look so good. One glimpse of you like this might scare your Ma half to death."

63

I said, "You don't look so good either."

"I don't feel so good." He smiled a little and winced. "I'm surprised I've got a face left. Oliver gave me some pretty good shots. It'd been a lot worse if you hadn't walloped Arlo over the noggin with that handle. How come you declared yourself into that fight?"

"It was so unfair. Both of them jumping on you."

"It was that, all right. I'd never have made it without your help. If I didn't thank you before, I do now. It was a nervy thing for a boy to do. All right, what say we wash up?"

The cold water felt mighty good. We sat on rocks side by side, washed our faces, and dabbed at cuts and bruises with soaked handkerchiefs. Mr. Chase finally looked me over and said, "You missed a couple of spots." He cleaned them up with his handkerchief. "There, you look some better. But not a whole lot. There's no doubt you've been in a slugfest. You ever had a black eye?"

"No," I said.

"You're going to now. How do I look?"

"Not so good. You missed quite a few." He sat still while I washed up his cuts. There were a couple of pretty bad ones. "That's the best I can do," I said finally. "You look like a mowing machine ran over you."

"I feel like it."

Then we just sat there saying nothing. I could feel the excitement of the fight draining out of me, even as it must have been from him. A kingfisher lit on a limb nearby and studied the water, then flew away. A faint breeze stirred the leaves. Mr. Chase looked up and smiled. The barrier between us was gone along with that small nagging fear. I was proud that I'd sided with him in the fight.

He asked, "You mind being called Chris? Your Ma always says Christopher."

"I like Chris better. Especially better than Boy," I said.

"Good. I don't like Mr. Chase. Frank suits me fine."

"Me, too," I said.

He wrung out his handkerchief in the creek again and stood up. "I doubt your Ma would have called this fight a practical thing. I figure she don't hold much with fightin'. Ladies mostly don't. You suppose she'll romp on us pretty hard?"

"A little, maybe," I said. "She didn't like Pa fighting, but she couldn't stop him. He had a temper."

"Mighty fine woman, your Ma," he observed. "Mighty fine. But she don't give an inch. Not a blessed inch."

"Pa always said she had a ramrod up her back," I said.

"That she has. Well, let's get these gladiators home. You know, the beatin' we get there may be worse than what Arlo and Oliver gave us."

THE MINUTE we walked through the door
Ma said, "Good heavens! What happened to you two?"

Ellie squinted up at my face and said, "Gee, Chris, does
it hurt?"

"A little," I said.

Frank Chase put the sack of flour carefully on the table.
I added my armload of supplies. Then he said casually,
"We had a little trouble in town."

"A little?" Ma was getting a pan and pouring hot water
into it. "What would you call a lot? And just what do you
mean by trouble? Are you going to tell me what happened
or do I start guessing?"

"You think you can?" Frank challenged.

Ma was soaking a towel and wringing it out. "Well,
Christopher's going to have a black eye and neither of you
got those bruises and scratches running into doors or

66

walls. They were caused by somebody's fists. I've seen the results before."

Frank winked at me. "I told you your Ma was a smart woman. Maybe she'll even tell us whose fists." He seemed unusually light-hearted.

"How many enemies do you have who'd do this to you?" Ma stopped wringing the towel and looked straight at Frank. "The Grayson brothers! But why?"

Frank shrugged. "Drunk again. Quarrelsome. And I was handy."

I said, "It wasn't that way at all, Ma. They followed him into Wright's store and picked on him. Oliver accused him of killing Pa and began beating up on him." I told her how Frank kept backing away from Oliver, how he tried to talk to him but it hadn't done any good. "And then Arlo jumped into the fight, too."

"Hold it right there, partner," Frank said. "You'd better let me tell that part." He did, and gave me a lot more credit than I deserved. "If Chris hadn't helped me out," he finished, "I'd have been beat to a pulp."

"You mean you're not now?" Ma asked. "You'd better look in a mirror." She wasn't excited or anything but her chin was set and there was color in her cheeks. "When is this going to end?" she asked. "Where was the Sheriff all this time?"

"I think this is the end," Frank said. "Sheriff Peck took 'em both to jail."

"Well, how did it end?" Ma asked. "Did the Sheriff stop them from killing you both? Did they beat you as bad as you look?"

"We weren't beat at all," I said getting excited again just thinking about it. "You should have seen what Frank did to that old Oliver Grayson. He was flat on his face when the Sheriff got there. I'll bet he eats soup for a week."

"I'll bet you do, too," Ma said dryly. "So you won?"

"We sure did," Frank said. "Chris had Arlo laid out cold with an ax handle."

"So, it's Chris and Frank now."

Frank nodded. "And long past time. We went through our baptism of fire shoulder to shoulder. That right, Chris?"

"We sure did," I said.

Ma said, "I see." Her lips had the faintest smile. Then she was all business. "I can't work on you standing up. Both of you sit down on this bench."

We sat side by side on the bench while she washed up our cuts and bruises with hot water and soap, then doused them liberally with peroxide.

Ellie peered closely at my eye and said, "Chris's eye is blue, Mom. It's just the skin that's black."

Frank said, "That's what's called a shiner, Baby."

I had some stiff muscles next morning, and I had a little trouble eating. Otherwise I felt fine. I noticed that Frank didn't move quite as spryly as usual and he was careful how he opened his mouth.

Ma fixed us lunches and right after breakfast we headed for our old place with the repaired wheel and rake teeth. It didn't take long to put the wheel on and fasten the teeth in place. Then I finished the raking. Frank began stacking the windrows into shocks ready to haul in.

When I finished raking I got a pitchfork and helped build shocks. But I wasn't as good at it as Frank. It was into the middle of the afternoon before we started loading. The sun was dropping close to the rim of the world when we finished.

Frank asked, "What time do the Fletcher horses go by?"

"Most any time now," I said.

"You want to hike up and see the blackie again?"

"I'm never going up there again," I said.

"That's plain foolish. You made a mistake and you learned by it. Come on, I'd like to get a look at that pony. We'll tie the team in the barnyard this time, give 'em some hay and they'll be all right."

I wanted to go, but I couldn't forget what had happened. "Suppose it was a bee. They could be stung down here, too."

"It's highly unlikely. Bees are up in the alfalfa and if you noticed there were a lot of flowers where you tied them before. Here in the barnyard there's not even a blade of grass. Nothing to attract bees."

"But you've seen that pony."

"Tied to a post rolling his eyes, waiting for somebody to try to ride him. I've never even seen that animal walk."

We tied the team securely to the barn timbers and gave each an armload of hay.

It didn't take long to climb the ridge. We settled side by side on the big flat rock. "This's all right!" Frank said. "You've got a grandstand view of the whole valley. They come past right underneath, eh?" He shaded his eyes looking off toward his land. "Didn't know the road made such a big curve. Man on horseback could save about a mile if he left the road at just about that big juniper and cut across country."

He was right. About halfway between our old place and town the road began a huge half circle that you were hardly aware of when you were traveling it.

We'd been there some fifteen or twenty minutes when I heard the familiar rumble of hoofs. "Here they come!"

I was suddenly on my knees with excitement. First there was the boil of dust churning straight up on the still air. Then they burst into view on top of the ridge, running hard. The sight, the drum of hammering hoofs, tossing manes and heads and flared nostrils, the dust drifting up toward us got me as it always did. The black pony was in the lead, mane and tail flying, head high, sharp ears forward, and eyes shining like polish stones. They passed beneath us, Fletcher's rider hazing them along.

When they were gone Frank Chase said, "By golly, he's some animal, for a fact! He's a real picture. I wanted to see him, to find out for myself what set you off. Now I know. Reminds me a little of that white one I was so crazy over when I was a kid. Couldn't blame a grown man for dreaming about this black, much less a boy. Too bad he's wild as a March hare. Did you notice that white rim around his eyes? The horse I liked didn't have that. He was a well-mannered, well-trained animal. Well"—he stood up—"guess we'd better be gettin' back."

We finished haying the next afternoon. The crop at our place wasn't as heavy as it was on Frank's.

After haying I rode Nellie over to our old place about every other day to water and hoe the garden. Watering brought on the weeds and it took a lot of hoeing. The bigger the corn and potato vines got the more water they took, and every drop had to be pumped by hand from about a hundred feet underground. It was sweat-popping work. But the garden was worth it. I was soon taking home a dozen or so ears of corn every other day and I kept Ma and Ellie busy shelling and canning beans. I purposely left early enough in the morning so I could climb the ridge and watch the black pony head out for pasture. I'm sure

Frank wouldn't have minded if I'd stayed late enough to see them return in the evening, but I didn't. Frank knew what I was doing. He asked once when we were alone in the barn, "How's the black pony? He still running the ridge?"

"Yes," I said.

Our six cows calved. We got four heifers and two bulls. All healthy, just as Ma predicted. Frank's cows added ten more but one was dead. It looked like we had calves running all over the place. The second cutting of alfalfa was coming on well. The first cutting had filled the barn jam-packed. We'd have to build the second and third into stacks in the field and put pole fences around them. Then in winter we could knock down the poles and let the cattle feed when the weather was bad.

Living had settled into a smooth operation. Frank was a good rancher. He knew the things that needed doing and he did them on time. We weren't flush with cash money, but neither were any of the homesteaders. But we were getting along well. It was slow because our herd of cattle was small and they were our money crop. We needed more cattle to sell but we'd have to raise our own.

There was no bickering or quarreling in the house. Ellie and I liked Frank. It bothered me some that I liked him more than I had Pa. But it was true. After the fight, I never had to worry that he'd blow up and yell and swear because I'd made some fool mistake. He took time to explain and help me. I enjoyed working with him.

We could have been one happy family but for Ma. I came to learn just how serious she'd been when she said that this would be a marriage of convenience. She still had that ramrod up her back and kept to her original declaration without giving an inch. The house stayed split right down the middle. When Frank was there she was careful never to step over that imaginary line. Only when he was out would she cross it as she went about keeping house.

Ellie paid no attention to it. I tried, until after that fight in town. Then I found myself crossing over without even thinking. Ma spoke to us about it a couple of times in private. Finally she ignored what we were doing. At first I felt a little guilty, as if I'd somehow let Ma down. But I got over that.

Every time Ma said "Mr. Chase" I felt embarrassed. She didn't forget for a second. For me, at least, there was an undercurrent of tension that kept this house and this family from becoming a home. I began to think that nothing would ever break it down.

We came home from church one Sunday and while we were eating dinner Ma asked, "Will we have plenty of hay for the stock this winter?"

"More than enough."

"Even with all the calves, the horses, and Fawn? There's fifteen calves that will be eating hay, you know."

"Don't worry. We'll even have hay to sell if we want to. The second cutting will be ready in another week or ten days. Both crops look good, at your place and here. And we'll get a third cutting, you know. We could feed more stock if we had it."

"Suppose we get a real hard winter?"

"I don't want to see a real hard one, of course. But we'd still have more than enough hay. Why?"

"I just wondered," Ma said. "Winter'll be coming soon."

"Not that soon, I hope." Frank smiled. "We've got a third cutting to get in."

"Time goes so fast," Ma said. "I just wanted to be sure. Harry almost didn't have enough for our few head last winter."

"Your alfalfa field was too young last year to bear heavy. It's now coming into its first good yield."

"Could you put in more alfalfa here?"

Frank nodded. "Eventually I'd like to put the whole three hundred acres in alfalfa and let the cattle run on the open range. There's a lot of it around here."

Ma said no more.

Next morning as Frank was getting ready to leave to cut poles for fencing around the haystacks Ma said, "Ellie and I are going with Christopher. We'll take the buggy. I'll have lunch all ready. All you'll have to do is warm it up. We'll be back in the afternoon."

Frank nodded and said, "Sure." He left with the ax over his shoulder.

"Do I get all dressed up?" Ellie was excited at the prospect of going somewhere.

"No," Ma said, "this isn't Sunday."

"Where we going, Mama?"

"Never mind. Just get your coat on. Christopher," Ma said, "bring the buggy around."

When I pulled up to the porch a few minutes later Ma and Ellie were waiting and Ma was dressed in her black Sunday best. I said, "You can't hoe corn and spuds in that dress."

"I don't intend to." Ma motioned Ellie into the buggy and climbed in after her.

I clucked to Nellie and we trotted out of the yard. "You told Frank you were going with me," I said, "and I'm going to our place for a load of corn to can."

73

"Not this morning," Ma said.

"Then where are we going?"

"To Sam Fletcher's. Do you know how to get there?"

"Sure," I said. "But why?"

"Christopher," she said, "I don't want to take the time to explain now. I want to think. If you'll be patient and listen when we get there you'll find out."

I was busting to ask questions but I knew better. Ma had that look about her that said she'd made up her mind about something and she was charging head-on straight into it.

8

It took over an hour to drive to Fletcher's. We had to go past our old place, then take a little-used road up over Christmas Ridge and down the other side into the next valley.

Fletcher's place was big and sprawling. He had half a dozen buildings, a big unpainted ranch house, and a maze of fences. There was stock grazing far as I could see.

Fletcher was coming from the barn as we drove into the yard. He took off his hat, smiled at Ma, and said, "Well, well, this is a surprise. How are you doing, Mrs. Fellows? I'm sorry," he said embarrassed, "I mean, Mrs. Chase. You know, habit's a terrible thing, ma'am. What do I owe this visit to?"

Ma ignored his slip of the tongue and said coolly, "Mr. Fletcher, if you have time I'd like to talk to you."

"All the time in the world." He smiled. "Come in the house."

75

Sam Fletcher was a bachelor and the house looked like it. There were no curtains at the windows or rugs on the floor. His parlor was a huge almost bare room. It held a big rough table and some chairs. A long line of bridles and coiled ropes hung from nails along one wall. A stretched-out cougar hide was nailed to the opposite wall.

"Won't you sit down," Mr. Fletcher asked. "Now, Mrs. Chase, what can I do for you?"

Ma said, "As you know, Mr. Fletcher, we're now living on the Chase place which is some two miles from our old home."

Fletcher nodded. "I know. Frank Chase is a good rancher. Knows his business."

"It's not practical for Mr. Chase to try to keep up two places," Ma said.

"Privately I've wondered about that."

"So, I've decided to sell our old place."

Those words hit me a real jolt and I looked quickly at Ma. She was sitting there very calm and quiet, looking straight at Fletcher. I knew then she had been arriving at this decision for some time.

Ellie, for once, didn't say a word. She just looked at Ma with her mouth open.

"I think you've made a wise decision," Fletcher said. "Is that what you wanted to talk to me about?"

"Exactly," Ma said. "I'd like to sell it to you."

"Oh." Fletcher took off his old hat and dropped it on the table. He ran fingers through his shock of white hair. "I thought you'd come to me for some advice."

"No," Ma said, "to sell."

"I see," he said. "I see. And what makes you think I might be interested in buying your place?"

"You approached my husband, Harry, about a year ago one day in town with an offer to buy."

Fletcher nodded. "So I did. I'd almost forgotten. Harry was complaining about being stuck out here on what he called this God-forsaken desert. He wanted to get away. I said I'd take it off his hands for a couple of hundred dollars, as I remember. Anyway enough to get him back East again. I think he'd have taken it but for you."

"I'm sure he would," Ma agreed. "Well, now you can have it."

"It seems to me I should be talking to Frank Chase about this. If I was interested in buying, that is, which I'm not."

"The land is mine free to sell. There was no agreement before my marriage to Mr. Chase. You should be interested in buying it."

"Why should I?" Fletcher asked. "It'll go back to the government like that of most of these other homesteaders who're goin' broke. If I still want it I can pick it up then for practically nothin'."

"My place is free and clear," Ma said. "We bought from a private party."

"I didn't know that," Fletcher said. "But I'll soon be able to get plenty of places around here for a little of nothin'. So why should I buy yours?"

"For the same reason you were interested a year ago," Ma said promptly. "Because it's very good valley bottomland."

"So's my own here, Mrs. Chase."

"Of course, but you have less than two hundred acres of good soil. The rest is hilly and good only for grazing."

"That's all I want it for."

"Naturally," Ma said, "you save your good bottomland for alfalfa hay like a good rancher should. You've got practically all of it planted now and you haven't enough to feed a thousand head through a hard winter. You need more good hay land and I have it."

"So, you're one of those smart women who knows all about ranching."

"No, but I was raised on a farm. I know good land. You haven't enough of it and we both know it."

"Like I said," Fletcher reminded her, "all I have to do is sit tight and I can pick up all the land I need when these settlers go broke. Good land, too."

"The people on the valley floor won't go broke. The others will."

"All these sod busters go belly up," Fletcher said disgustedly. "They think rainfall follows the plow. They're learning the hard way it don't. These schoolteachers and store clerks are gonna go busted as sure as shootin'."

"Most will," Ma agreed. "But the valley floor is not dryland farming. Those people aren't store clerks and teachers. They're mostly good farmers. They looked the land over and knew what they were getting. They'll make it."

"You've got a long head for a lady."

"So have you," Ma said. "That's why you're the most prosperous cattleman around. And that's why you should be interested in my three hundred acres. You need more hay land. And good land, such as mine, is always scarce."

"I've got by without it so far," Fletcher said.

"You've been lucky. Your herd's got bigger the past two years and we've had open winters. Cattle could do very well rustling for themselves. We're due for a hard winter any time. That means you'll have to feed hay, a lot of it. And you haven't enough good hay land to raise the hay you'll need any winter now. You need more good land and you need it now. One hard winter without enough feed and you could lose half your stock. Then you'd be little better off than the rest of us."

Fletcher studied Ma with bright little eyes. "You would make a successful rancher, Mrs. Chase. I admit I've thought that way for some time now and have had my weather fingers crossed. But there are other places besides yours. I've been watching a number of them, just waiting."

"Mine is the only one within five miles of you that's available now," Ma said. "And five miles is too far to haul hay or care for another place. Mine is just over the ridge, a little less than an hour's haul. It has a serviceable barn, fences, a good house with a deep well. You can put a family over there to care for the place. That is worth something, Mr. Fletcher."

Fletcher considered. "You have a point, Mrs. Chase. You've figured my situation out to a T. There's no sense our beating around the bush about it. I will take your place if we can come to a reasonable figure."

"Four dollars an acre," Ma said promptly.

"I said a reasonable figure, Mrs. Chase."

"That's dirt cheap."

"Not out here where I can buy homestead land for a dollar twenty-five an acre."

"Upland desert fit only for summer grazing and jack rabbits. I'm talking about valley floor soil, with buildings, fences, and ten acres of alfalfa already in. That's another plus."

"Still too high if you wanta sell."

"Want to," Ma said, "don't have to. I can hold it indefinitely or advertise in the Eastern papers where I'm sure I can sell it. Then you will have missed a fine piece of land that is just next door."

"Perhaps you'd better advertise it back East."

"I considered it," Ma said. "But that will take time. I can use the money now if we can strike a bargain."

Mr. Fletcher drummed stubby fingers on the table top watching Ma closely. "Tell you what I'll do, Mrs. Chase. I'll give you two fifty an acre right now, today. That's seven hundred fifty dollars cash money on the barrel head."

"Not enough," Ma said. "I'm sure I can get the four dollars by advertising in the East. I'm not offering unimproved desert land, you know."

"That will not be clear money," Fletcher pointed out. "You'll have to pay a commission." He dug fingers through his hair, annoyed. "I've never done business with a woman."

"Man or woman, a deal is a deal," Ma said. "It's my land to sell. And I won't pay a commission. Just the price of an ad, a few dollars."

"You're mistaken if you think you can sell it that way."

"You're mistaken if you think I can't. I'm from the East. I know. The papers are full of ads every day for land out here."

"You're sharper than most men. I'd rather deal with a man any day. I'll give you three dollars and believe me that's out of the bigness of my heart, because I'm doing business with a woman."

"I appreciate your thoughtfulness," Ma said, "but it's the value of my land we're discussing. Not me."

"In that case three dollars," Fletcher said promptly.

"I'm willing to sacrifice some rather than spend the time and bother of advertising in the East," Ma said. "I'll come down to three seventy-five."

Fletcher shook his head. "You heard me, three dollars."

"Have you stopped to figure what it would cost you to lose say five hundred head in a blizzard or have them lose twenty-five or thirty percent of their weight for lack of feed? You'd be lucky to get out of it with a loss of only several thousand dollars. Now if you owned my place and had feed you'd save that stock and that weight loss. Calculate that into dollars and you'd be getting my place for nothing several times over."

"Lady, you're way ahead of me," Fletcher said. "I don't follow that kind of reasoning. Now I'll tell you what I will do, I'll give you three dollars and twenty-five cents an acre and that is positively my last offer. You can take that or advertise in your Eastern paper and try to sell it. I'm betting that you don't."

"I would sell it," Ma said, "but I'll take it providing we get the food from the garden Christopher planted this spring and the next two cuttings of alfalfa."

"The vegetables and such I don't want," Fletcher said. "But I want that third cutting of alfalfa."

"Sold," Ma said promptly.

"You're a mighty sharp bargainer," Fletcher said.

"You got a fine piece of land, good buildings, and a well. It's less than we paid and we improved it."

"You paid too much. But no matter. When you bring me your deed I'll have your money ready."

"I'll bring it tomorrow," Ma promised.

"Now that we've made the deal," Fletcher said. "Tell

me, do you really think you could have sold it yourself by advertising?"

"Who knows? It only takes one party to make a sale."

"I must remind myself to never do business with a woman again," Fletcher said.

We went back to the buggy. I couldn't believe it. In a few minutes Ma had sold our farm for cash to Sam Fletcher who was known as one of the sharpest dealers in the whole valley.

"Now," Ma said, "drive over to the Hamilton ranch. Do you know where it is?"

I said, "Sure. I went to school with Dan Hamilton."

Ma didn't say a word on the drive. She sat straight and prim and it seemed to me well satisfied with herself. I didn't talk either. It wouldn't have done any good to ask questions. Ellie chattered a little about a bird she saw and a rabbit but no one answered so she quit.

At the Hamiltons' Ma left Ellie and me in the buggy and went in alone. She wasn't gone more than five minutes. "Now," she said, "we'll go home. You can stop at the garden on the way and get some corn." She was smiling a kind of pleased smile that I hadn't seen in a long time.

It didn't take but a few minutes to break off a sack of corn and stuff it in the back of the buggy.

When we reached home Frank had been in, had lunch, and was gone again.

After we'd eaten I husked out the corn and spent the rest of the afternoon helping Ma and Ellie can it. I was dying to ask what had gone on at the Hamiltons' and why she'd decided to sell our old place but I knew she'd tell me when she got ready.

That night after we'd had supper and the dishes were washed Ma said to Frank, "There's something you should know. I didn't go to our old place today to help Christopher."

"I figured that."

"Oh?" Ma looked surprised.

"Chris doesn't need help to gather a sack of corn or do a little watering. And this time of year with the corn so high and the potatoes and the rest growing so well there's very little hoeing."

Ma said, "We went to see Sam Fletcher."

"I'd never have guessed that."

"I sold my place to him."

"Sold it! To Sam Fletcher!" Frank leaned back in his chair.

"It wasn't practical for you to try to work two places a couple of miles apart. The money could be better used for other things."

"Could that be the reason you asked if we'd have enough hay for winter and if I could plant more alfalfa here?"

Ma nodded. She explained the deal she'd made with Fletcher and then why we'd gone to the Hamiltons'. "Judy Hamilton told me at church Sunday that they're broke and are going to leave. Did you know that?"

Frank shook his head. "I knew they were having trouble."

"They plan to have a public sale in a couple of weeks and sell off everything. They have twenty head of cattle. I agreed to buy them this morning at twenty dollars a head." Ma sat very straight at the table on her side of the house, head high, hands flat on the table top while she talked. Her cheeks were flushed, from the heat of the stove probably, and her gray eyes were bright in the reflection of the oil lamp.

Frank Chase sat at his end of the table and listened, half smiling and nodding.

"We'll get an additional twenty head of stock and have five hundred seventy-five dollars to put in the bank to use to buy more stock or whatever we need," Ma finished.

"That's amazing," Frank said. "Simply amazing. Particularly selling to Sam Fletcher. He's a mighty sharp man, very close with a dollar."

"Then you approve?"

"Absolutely. I'm sorry you thought it necessary to get rid of your place. But you're right. It would have been hard to keep up both."

"We'll have to plant more alfalfa here," Ma said.

"I'll put in another twenty or twenty-five acres next spring. I've got a couple of hundred in the bank to add to your five seventy-five. We'll have some steers to market next spring. Why, we'll have cash money to buy more stock."

Ellie said, "Mr. Fletcher said Mama had a long head. It looks the same to me."

Frank laughed. "He meant your mother's a smart woman, Baby." He shook his head. "Poor old Sam Fletcher. I can almost feel sorry for him. Why, he didn't have any more chance than a rabbit with a broken leg cornered by a pack of hungry coyotes. Once your Mother started in on him with her practical logic he was sunk."

"I told him the truth," Ma said.

"Of course. It's the way you lay it out that gets a man. He doesn't expect that kind of logic from a woman."

84

I said, "When we get Hamilton's twenty cattle you'll only be nine hundred and twenty-six short."

"That's right."

"What does that mean?" Ma asked.

Frank looked at me, then at Ma. I could see he was just busting to tell her. "Why not?" he said. There was sudden excitement in his voice. "Why not?" He was on his feet pacing back and forth and his voice had a lift like I'd never heard. "The first time I saw this land I knew it was what I'd been looking for all my life. I could see it all in hay and grain and a thousand head of my own stock roaming the open range around here. I'll still be nine hundred and twenty-six short. But they're coming! By golly, they're coming!" He stopped and smiled, a little embarrassed. "The boy and his dream," he said.

"Why not?" Ma agreed quietly. "As Christopher says, you're only nine hundred and twenty-six short."

Frank just looked at her for what seemed the longest time then he said, "That first day you told me that in a month or so I'd wonder how I'd got along without you. You were right. You were dead right."

Ma smiled. Then she rose. "Ellie, time for bed. Christopher, have you turned Fawn out yet?"

"No," I said.

Frank went out with me. I turned Fawn into the pasture and he let out Gyp and Jess. Fawn wandered off and began to eat. The horses lay down, rolled, then got up and shook themselves. They moved off into the dark.

Frank and I leaned on the gate and looked at the night. It was warm and quiet. The growing alfalfa was a pungent mustiness on the night air. I thought of the black pony. Our old place would be sold tomorrow. As soon as the garden was harvested I'd have no reason to go over there. I wouldn't see the pony again. I felt a sense of great loss.

Beside me Frank said, "You know, your Ma is an amazing woman. Yes siree, Bob. An amazing woman."

"I guess so," I said.

He scowled down at me from his lean height. "You guess so? I know so, Boy," he said positively.

Lying in bed later I thought about the amazing things that had happened that day. Selling our old place had been a shock, but not too great. This was home now. Anybody could see that Frank was pleased and that he liked Ma. I thought of Ma telling Frank what she'd done and how she'd looked and I came up with my own reasons for her doing what she had. It was her way of beginning to unbend. She was being won over by Frank Chase just like Ellie and I were. I was sure now that soon the undercurrent of formality that split the house down the middle would be gone. Everything was turning out just right. I went to sleep feeling mighty good.

Next morning Ma and I went to Fletcher's with all the necessary papers, turned them over to him, and were back home by noon with his check for nine hundred seventy-five dollars. It was the largest check I'd ever seen.

That afternoon Frank and I went to the Hamiltons' and drove the twenty head of cattle home. I rode Nellie and he rode Jess. The cattle seemed in good shape.

We turned them into the pasture and Ma and Ellie came out. We all leaned over the fence and watched them wander off to join our little herd.

Frank put an arm over Ma's shoulders and said happily, "Thanks to you we now have about the biggest cattle outfit this side of Christmas Ridge. That was a great thing you did, Mabel."

Ma moved away so that his arm fell to his side. Her voice was as firm as I'd ever heard it. "It was the practical thing to do. We both know that."

I glanced at her quickly. She was completely cool and composed. She turned and walked toward the house, her head high, her back rigid. Nothing had changed.

I GUESS at twelve a boy's disappointments aren't all-consuming. I felt bad that Ma wasn't more unbending. It would have made our home life more pleasant. Then we went to mowing the second cutting of alfalfa and it was pushed into the back of my mind.

The second crop on both places was better than the first. We spent almost two weeks cutting, raking, hauling it in, and building it into big wigwam-shaped stacks. It took the better part of another week to put the pole fences around the stacks to keep the cattle out until we were ready for winter feeding.

After that I went back to our old place again, now Sam Fletcher's, to take care of my garden. Fletcher hadn't put anyone on the place yet. I had quite a bit of watering to do. Carrots and a few other vegetables were coming on and I had to keep the potatoes hilled. We still got a few nubbins of corn for the table.

I'd ride over on Nellie. I went oftener than was absolutely necessary so I could climb the ridge to watch the black pony running out to pasture. Once I finished with the garden there'd be no reason to go and I'd never see the pony again.

Sam Fletcher came to the house one evening to see Frank. "I want to build a loafing shed," he said. "If you've got the time I could use you for two or three weeks." We were between the second and third cutting of alfalfa and Frank had time. He rode Jess over and back. That left me taking care of most things at home between going to our old place to tend my garden.

One evening about a week later, I'd let Fawn into the barn to milk her and was heading up to the house for the milk pail when Frank rode into the yard. I stopped and just stared at him. I couldn't believe what I was seeing. Ma and Ellie had come out on the porch and they, too, were standing and staring.

Frank had been riding Jess bareback all week, but tonight he had a saddle. The reason was obvious. Of all things! he was leading on a halter rope Fletcher's black pony. The pony was pulling back, fighting the rope. His head was high as it always was. His sharp ears jumped back and forth. His nostrils flared and he kept snorting. His eyes had that wild look as if he was about to explode in all directions any second.

Frank said quietly, "Open the barn door, Chris. Then stand out of the way."

I ran and opened the door. Ma and Ellie hurried down to see what it was all about.

Frank nudged Jess forward and the pony followed dancing sideways, snorting and pulling against the rope all the way. Frank rode through the barn door. But the pony braced his front legs and refused to budge. Frank kept the pressure on and called to me, "Get a switch or something and cut him across the legs. But be sure to stand clear."

A length of rope was draped over the fence. I took that and cut the pony sharply across the legs. He jumped inside with a startled snort and I slammed the door.

Frank dismounted slowly, talking to the pony all the time in a low voice. He pulled him into Jess's stall and tied him. Then he took off his hat and wiped his forehead. "Whew! I'm glad that's over. A couple of times I didn't think I was going to make it home with him."

I was frantic to ask questions, but just then Ma and Ellie came through the door. Ma folded her arms and looked at the pony critically. He kept stamping back and forth, snorting and pulling on the rope and showing the whites of his eyes.

Ellie was first to say anything. "Gee," she said, "he sure is black. Where'd you get him, Daddy Frank?"

"I'd like to know that, too," Ma said. "And what's he doing here?"

"He belonged to Sam Fletcher," Frank said. "He was one of the bunch that ran the ridge every day."

"What do you mean, belonged?" Ma asked suspiciously.

"He's Chris's pony now."

"Fletcher gave him to you?"

"Not exactly. I traded labor for him."

"How much labor?"

"Ths past week."

"You traded a whole week's hard labor for this animal? A horse we have absolutely no use for?"

"Maybe we haven't, but Chris has."

"What possible use?" Ma demanded. "He's got Nellie to ride or have you forgotten?"

"Of course not." Frank explained lamely, "This is the pony Chris wants."

Ma looked at Frank, then at me. Her lips were tight. There were spots of angry color in her cheeks. "It seems there's something here I don't know about."

I couldn't let Frank take any more blame. I told her how I'd been climbing the ridge all spring and summer just to watch him pass.

Ma listened without saying a word. When I finished she said, "I can understand you wanting your own horse. I guess every boy does. But we certainly don't need this one. He'll be eating hay and oats and taking up needed space in the barn. An animal we have absolutely no need for." She spread her hands. "It doesn't make sense. Why, it's, it's . . ."

"Impractical," Frank said quietly.

"Exactly! It's the most impractical thing I can think of."

"I don't agree," Frank answered.

"Oh, you don't." Ma's head was high, her voice was sharp. "We're struggling from hand to mouth to make a go of this place. I even sold my ranch to try to help out. Then you work a solid week, and take this animal for pay. It'd been better if you'd worked for nothing. Then, at least, we wouldn't have had to feed it."

Frank shook his head. "I understand how you feel, and you're absolutely right. But a boy should have a few things he wants and dreams about. I wanted a horse more than anything in the world at Chris's age. I didn't get it and it was one of the tragedies of my life. I don't want Chris to feel the way I did. But I didn't go to work for Fletcher with the idea of getting him, if that's what you're thinking. It happened suddenly tonight."

"What happened?" Ma asked.

"They brought these horses into the corral," Frank explained. "Fletcher had hired a new rider that day who thought he was pretty good. He bet he could ride any horse there and they chose this one. The animal threw him and broke his leg. That made Fletcher killing mad. He needed the rider bad and he ran into the house for a rifle. He was going to shoot the pony." Frank looked at me. "I couldn't see him kill the pony you loved so I offered to trade my labor for the week for him and Fletcher took it."

"It was his horse," Ma pointed out. "He had every right to do whatever he wanted. Not that I'd have been in favor of shooting him." She was studying the pony thoughtfully, biting at the end of her finger. "He bucked, you say. I've seen this animal before. Of course." She snapped her fingers. "The Fourth of July last year. Fletcher's bucking horse that everybody was trying to ride. Nobody could ride him. They called him an outlaw. Fletcher kept him for that purpose. He wouldn't shoot a good horse even if a man did break a leg. But Fletcher wasn't losing a thing by shooting this one." She looked straight at Frank. "He robbed you of a week's wages. You've bought a horse that no one in this valley would have taken as a gift. I'll bet Fletcher's laughing up his sleeve right now. And so will the valley when they hear about it."

"I don't care what the valley thinks," Frank said.

Ma turned on me. "You couldn't want a respectable animal like Nellie or Gyp or Jess. You had to have a no-good, half-wild outlaw. Well, he's your problem now, young man. You'd better make him good for something around here besides eating valuable feed." She grabbed Ellie's hand and whisked out of the barn.

Frank looked after her. "I've never seen her this mad and I can't blame her. But when Fletcher came out of the house with the rifle I couldn't help thinking how I'd have felt if somebody had shot that white horse I wanted so bad. I couldn't let it happen."

"I'm glad you didn't," I said. I started to pat the satiny flank and like a flash he swung away and slammed against the opposite side of the stall.

"He's mighty wild and skittish," Frank said. "You've got your work cut out gentling him."

I studied the pony standing there head high, twisted around watching me with that wild look. He was ready to jump or let fly with both hind feet the moment I touched him. "I thought to gentle any animal you had to approach them, to pet them," I said. "I can't even get close to him. I don't know how to begin."

Frank scratched his head. "I'm no expert. I'm about like every other rancher. I can break the average horse to ride or work but that's about it. One thing I can tell you about this animal; you'll have to take it mighty slow and careful. Don't get too close behind him until he's gentled some. He could kick your head off. And don't get in the stall with him. He could crowd you against the wall and crush you."

"If I can't pet him or curry him or even work around him, what can I do?" I asked.

"Offhand I'd say not much. For you the most important thing to start with is to understand what made him this way. It was men. In trying to ride him he's been hog-tied, beat, blindfolded, snubbed tight to a post, and no telling what else. You can bet that everything that can be done to an animal he's suffered, so you can't blame him for not trusting anybody. Your first job is to try to get his confidence. That won't be easy. You'll need a world of patience. Don't lose your temper with him no matter what he does. Remember why he does it."

"How do I go about getting his confidence?"

"We'll leave him in the barn a few days. Hang around his general vicinity. Let him get used to seeing you. He'll soon learn he doesn't have to get ready for a fight the minute you show up. Feed him, water him from a bucket. Talk to him. In a couple of days he'll know that he has to depend on you to eat and drink. He's smart. That's why he became an outlaw. Men have cultivated the fighting streak in him because they learned he had one. You've got to try to counteract that. There's one big thing on your side. Horses like human companionship. They want the love and attention of people. You've got to work on that. And another thing; you've got to outthink this fellow at every step." Frank stopped and studied the pony who kept snorting delicately, swinging his head, stamping back and forth. "I knew he was a bucker, but I didn't realize he was this bad until we started home. He fought me every step of the way. I sure haven't given you an easy job. Your Ma was dead right. Buying him was pretty stupid. But if I had it to do over, even knowing what I do now about him, I'd still do it. Give him some hay and let's go in to supper, that is, if your Ma will let us in the house."

I got a big armload of hay and Frank said, "Give him a third of that. Feed him a little at a time but feed him often. That way he'll come to rely on you. To start with you have to reach him through his stomach."

I put a small amount in the manger then stepped back and watched him. He came forward a step at a time. Still watching me with those big liquid eyes, he put his head down and got a mouthful. I wanted to reach out and touch him so bad I could almost taste it. I said to Frank, "I'll do everything I can to tame him. But even if I can't and can never ride him I'm glad you bought him. Thanks."

Frank said, "I guess we're a couple of impractical darned fools. Come on, let's go."

I went out to milk after supper and the pony had eaten the hay. I got a little more, carried it to the manger, and said, "So you ate it all. Here's some more." He backed up the length of the halter rope and watched me. I dropped the hay and said, "Relax, take it easy. I'm not going to hurt you. You're going to see a lot of me, so you might as well get used to it."

I milked Fawn and turned her out into the pasture. When I left the barn the pony was eating.

I strained the milk and put it in pans to let the cream rise. Then I returned to the barn. I sat down in the hay a few feet in front of the manger and watched the pony eating. I'd dreamed about him so long and wanted him so much it was like a pain every time I thought of him. And now here he was, in our barn, in front of me eating hay and he was mine, all mine. I wanted to reach out and touch that soft nose, run my hands down the satiny black neck to prove I wasn't dreaming. I didn't even think of riding him, not then. I just wanted to love him and care for him. I knew it would take time for the pony to get used to me and learn to like having me around. A terrible impatience welled up inside me. I didn't see how I could wait for tomorrow.

THINGS AT HOME were certainly not the way I wanted them and it was partly my fault. Besides splitting the house down the middle and holding rigidly to her rules about this marriage of convenience, Ma was stiff-necked toward me. I couldn't blame her. We had always been very close but now I could feel the distance between us growing wider than the top of Christmas Ridge. I didn't know what to do about it. I couldn't tell Frank to take the pony back to Sam Fletcher. He'd worked a week without pay to get the animal for me. I was sure that giving me the pony was a little like slipping backward through time to when he'd been a boy and dreamed about a certain white horse. It was like making his dream come true. I couldn't spoil that. But I certainly didn't like the gulf developing between Ma and me. At moments I wished I'd never heard of the pony but the next minute I wouldn't give him up for anything. I was real mixed up.

I tried to follow Frank's advice, fed the pony, talked quietly to him, stayed close where he could get used to seeing me. But I didn't handle him in any way.

Frank returned to work at Fletcher's. The job would last two or three more weeks. I went to our old place about every third day so there was plenty of time to be around the black pony. I spent a lot of it watering and feeding him small amounts of hay and a little oats. I sat in the hay in front of him and talked in a low intimate voice. He got so he'd stand and watch me with those big dark eyes. The way those sharp ears pricked forward I was sure he was listening. Once I tried to reach out and touch his face but he jerked his head away.

About the third day I tried to hand feed him. I let him eat all the hay in the manger then I talked to him several minutes to get him good and quiet. "You're sure no good for anything the way you are. I've got to make you useful for something but you've got to help me. I don't blame Ma for not wanting you. If I can break you to ride, maybe pull a buggy, she might change her mind about you. But I can't do it alone. I'm not going to hurt you. You've got to understand that. Now, let's you and me get started knowing each other." I held out a handful of hay. He backed off, snorting delicately. "Come on," I said, "it's just hay. You know that. There's nothing to be afraid of."

"Maybe he wants something else. Hay's all he's been getting the past three days."

I had no idea how long Ma had been standing behind me. I said, a little embarrassed, "Frank said I should talk to him, that it'd help him get over being afraid or nervous."

"Of course," Ma agreed, "and as long as he is nervous you should tempt him with food he knows is mouth-watering."

"If I had some sugar cubes," I said.

"He wouldn't know a sugar cube from a stone so he wouldn't touch it. Now, if you had a carrot. You brought some home the other day. Run up to the house and get three or four good juicy ones with tops on."

I ran and got the carrots. Ma held one at arm's length and moved slowly up to the manger. She said quietly, "This isn't hay. You know this is good. Come and get it. You know you want it. I've seen your kind before. My father was very good at handling horses like you. Come on."

The pony looked at the carrot, snorted and tossed his head. But he stayed the length of the halter rope away. Finally he came up a step at a time, stretched his neck, lifted the carrot, and ate it greedily.

Ma put another carrot in the feed box. He ate that. The third she held at arm's length. "Come on," she coaxed. "Take it."

He came a step at a time, stretched his neck, and nibbled at the green top. Ma handed me the last one and said, "You do the same. No more."

I held out the carrot. He took it.

"There," Ma said. "Step number one. Take your time and work slow and easy. This animal has been abused plenty."

"Can I give him some more?" I asked.

"A few, but go easy. We need them for this winter. Those cornstalks at our old place should have some sweet juicy suckers down near the ground. Why don't you bring some home for him?" She studied the pony. "Have you named him?"

"I've just been calling him the black pony. You got any ideas?" I asked hopefully, thinking that maybe she was beginning to give a little.

"A couple," she said. "My father had a horse like this once. He didn't keep him long though. He called him Satan." Her lips had become straight and tight. "That certainly fits this animal. Or you could call him Useless. That fits, too."

I said, "I'm sorry, Ma. I'm awfully sorry."

"So am I." She leaned against a post and folded her arms. "It would be different if we were well off. You know how we're scratching and scrimping to get ahead. Right now we need every bit of feed and every penny we can scrape up. The hay this animal eats could save several heifers or fatten a couple of steers. I don't have to tell you that could mean vitally important cash."

"I didn't dream Frank would ever get him," I said. "He did it for me. If I turned him down now it'd be like—like a slap in the face."

"And you don't want to turn him down."

"No," I said miserably.

Ma walked to the door. The gulf between us was wider than ever. "You don't like calling him Satan. All right, how about calling him Lucifer? It's not very original but it fits. It fits in more ways than you know."

"How do you mean?"

"Lucifer was an angel, but he led a revolt of the angels in heaven and fell from grace. Then he became known as Satan."

"But he had been an angel," I said.

"That's right. I doubt you can make an angel out of this animal but you can try." She went out and closed the door.

Right then I'd have given almost anything if I'd never heard of the black pony.

For several days I tried a variety of names on him but for some reason Lucifer stuck. Maybe I couldn't make an angel of him but at least I could try.

Ma always said you climbed a mountain one step at a time. My first step was to get those fresh, tender green corn suckers and a few more carrots from the garden.

I fed him the carrots first. Since he'd tasted them and wanted more he took every one from my hand. Then I started in on the corn suckers. He took them, too. I kept talking to him. I talked about everything, school and harvesting hay, the trouble between Ma and me that he was to blame for, what a good pony I was going to make of him, and a lot more I don't remember. Anything to keep him listening to my voice.

Soon he'd stand quietly munching suckers while I fed them to him one at a time. Finally, still talking and feeding him with one hand, I reached out and put the other on his neck. It felt like silk. I ran my hand up and scratched carefully at the base of his ears. He stopped eating and stood perfectly still, but he didn't jerk his head away. I wanted to do more but I was afraid to push my luck. I dropped my hand and fed him the last corn sucker. Excitement was boiling in me. I said, "You don't know it, but you and I are going to be great friends and I'm going to ride you. You can count on it."

When Frank came home I told him and he said, "Good, let's try taking him out and let him drink from the trough. Maybe we can let him get a little exercise in the corral." He tied a lariat to the end of the halter rope then carefully backed Lucifer out of the stall. The instant he saw the open door he bolted for it. He made it into the corral and there Frank snubbed him to the big snubbing post sunk deep into the ground.

He fought the post for a few minutes but Frank kept talking quietly to him and he soon quieted down. Then Frank led him to the trough and because he was plenty thirsty he drank. Afterward Frank stayed close to the post so he could take a fast wrap around it. He let out the lariat almost to the end and Lucifer circled, snorting and dancing and tossing his head, getting his first exercise since he'd come here. I didn't know anyone else was around until Ellie said, "Gee, he sure is pretty running, isn't he, Mama?"

Ma and Ellie were watching through the poles of the corral.

"Yes," Ma said, "he's pretty."

Frank let him circle until he began to sweat, then he shortened up on the lariat and took him back into the barn.

That was the pattern of the next couple of days. By then I could walk right in and pet him and he stood quietly.

Then the corn suckers gave out. That evening Frank let me back Lucifer out and lead him to the watering trough. He drank long and steadily and I stood beside him, a hand on his glistening neck, proud as the king of Siam. When he finished he turned his head and those nostrils sucked in a good long breath of me. Then he blew mightily showering me.

Frank laughed. "I think you've got a friend. I told you he was smart. Try leading him around."

I walked him around the corral and he was at my heels

like a dog. After the third lap Frank said, "Take him inside and tie him and we'll see how he reacts to currying and brushing."

He jumped at the first touch of the currycomb. After that he loved it. I'm sure he'd never been curried before.

"Take him out tomorrow," Frank said. "Do it two or three times and walk him around the corral but be sure the gate and barn door are closed. Don't try riding him, understand?"

"When can I try?"

"I don't know. We're going to take this a day at a time." He stuck a straw in his mouth and studied Lucifer. "Riding him could be a long way off, if ever."

"But look how tame he's got in a few days."

"Walking up to him, petting him, leading him around, currying and feeding him is one part, the simple part. He likes that. Riding him is something else again. The second a man hits his back he'll remember spurs and whip and yelling and excitement. That's when he'll start to fight. It's all he's ever known. They tell me he's piled up most of the best riders in the valley. So you stay off him until I give the word. Concentrate on getting his confidence and friendship and nothing else."

I worked on that. I walked him around and around the corral, fed him the choicest bits of hay, curried and brushed him until his coat glistened, and talked to him by the hour. When I went to our old place to hoe and water the garden I took him along. I walked the whole distance because I was afraid to try leading him and riding Nellie. I had no trouble. He paced along beside me as docile as could be turning his head every so often to blow his breath at me and, finally, to nibble delicately at my shirt with his lips.

When we returned Ma asked, "Did you have any trouble?"

"No," I said. "He was as tame as Nellie."

"Don't be fooled by that, Christopher," she said sharply. "Don't trust that pony."

"But, Ma, Ellie could have led him."

"I don't care. Don't you trust him."

The next day we headed out across country onto the open range. It was warm. We dropped into a small valley where the grass was lush and the creek made a wide bend nearby. I held the halter rope and Lucifer fed a circle around me seeming completely content. Then I decided to try something. I dropped the rope and let him go. He kept ripping out grass. When he wandered off I went over and picked up the rope again. He just lifted his head with a mouthful and looked at me. I dropped the rope, stretched out in the shade of a bush and looked up at the cloudless sky. It was utterly still except for the steady snipping of grass, the hum of bees, and a single meadowlark's clear voice. I must have gone to sleep because I became conscious with a start. Lucifer was standing over me blowing his breath in my face. I knew then I'd never have to worry about him running away from me.

For the first time I thought seriously about riding him. If I could ride up to the house Ma would realize he was a good working pony, a valuable addition to have on the place, one who'd earn his keep. Then, I told myself, she'd get over her peeve at me and that wide void between us would be gone. I thought about it all the way home and I especially thought about it lying in bed that night.

The next afternoon we returned to the same spot. It seemed like such a logical thing to ride him today. It would be a wonderful surprise. I let him feed for a while figuring a full stomach would somehow help. Then I picked up the dragging halter rope. I petted him and rubbed his ears and talked to him. "They say you're an outlaw. I don't believe it. When we ride up to the house we'll prove it to Ma. We'll prove it to the whole valley. You know me. You know I wouldn't hurt you for anything." I ran my hand along his sleek back where I'd sit. He glanced around, then calmly went on eating. I petted him some more. Then I led him to a rock that jutted a couple of feet above ground. It would be easy to mount from there. I stepped up on the rock, got a good grip on his mane and said, "Easy, boy," lifted my leg over his back and carefully slipped on.

He looked around, surprised. The next instant his ears were back and his head down. I'm not exactly sure what happened next but I was sailing through the air and I'd lost my grip on the halter rope. I think I turned a complete somersault. I landed with a bone-jarring crash flat on my stomach and began plowing up the sod with my face. It shook me up plenty and knocked the wind out of me. I lay there for maybe half a minute getting my breath back and feeling for broken arms and legs. Everything seemed all right. I turned over and sat up.

Lucifer stood about ten feet away head down, looking at me curiously. I got up, picked up the halter rope and led him back to the rock. He seemed perfectly calm. I'd mounted too slow, I told myself, given him too much time to think about it and be ready for me. I petted him again and talked quietly to him. Then I stepped to the rock and onto his back in one quick motion. Before I was even settled he seemed to explode under me. His back was humped, his head down between his feet. I think I stuck for about three jumps then we parted company. I plowed into the ground again but this time I was ready for the shock and it didn't seem to hurt quite so much. Once again Lucifer just stood there, ears pricked forward, watching me curiously. I didn't get up quite as fast, but I did get up. I meant to try again.

Lucifer tossed me twice more. The last time I don't remember landing. I must have been knocked out for a minute or two. When I came to I was lying flat on my back and something wet was running down the side of my face. I raised my hand and felt stickiness. Then I looked at my fingers. Blood! I turned my head. Lucifer was calmly eating grass about twenty feet away. I sat up gingerly and then I saw the small rock. Apparently I'd hit my head on it when I landed.

I started to get up and fell back with a groan. My right ankle wouldn't support me. I could feel my foot swelling inside the shoe. I got the shoe and sock off and looked at it. It throbbed like a toothache and was already beginning to puff. I couldn't move the ankle and there was no way to tell if it was broken or not. I pulled the sock on but already I couldn't get the shoe on. I wasn't going to walk home on that foot.

Lucifer wandered over, nickered, and put his head down and blew his breath in my face. I patted his head and said, "You sure fixed me up good. We're in real trouble now and we're both to blame. I shouldn't have tried to ride you, but you had no call to buck me off. Ma's going to throw a grade-A conniption fit for sure this time. But it'll be tougher on you because she's dead against you anyway." I sat there aching and feeling very bad the way this had turned out. Lucifer wandered off and began eating grass again.

My foot and ankle were on fire. If I could get to the

creek and soak it in cold water. And I must have a lot of blood and dirt on my face that needed washing off. I explored for the gash on my head and found it very near the hairline. It had almost stopped bleeding.

It was about a quarter mile to the creek. Maybe if I could find a broken limb I could use for a crutch. But we were almost in the middle of the little meadow. The first brush was a couple of hundred yards off and that was low and scrawny. Maybe I could hold to Lucifer's mane and hobble to the creek.

I crawled to the rock I'd used for mounting, pulled myself into a sitting position on top of it and called Lucifer. He came to me. I gathered up the halter rope, took hold of his mane with the other hand and pulled myself upright. I tried to touch my foot to the ground to help. Pain cut like a knife. I held to his mane and began to hop. I managed about a dozen hops then sank down to the ground again. I'd have to wait right here until Ma or Frank came looking for me.

I glanced at the sun. It would be a good three hours before they missed me enough to begin worrying and come looking. Lucifer went back to eating grass, wandering idly back and forth near me. I held my handkerchief to my head until the bleeding stopped. My head finally quit aching but my ankle was giving me fits. It seemed like the sun took forever going down, but finally long shadows spread across the ground and the cool of evening began driving the heat away.

Frank rode down into the meadow on Nellie. He spotted Lucifer and came over. He slid off and bent over me. "Well," he said, "you're kind of messed up. Don't bother telling me what happened. I'll tell you. You tried to ride

Lucifer after I told you not to unless I was there. Why?"

"He seemed so tame. I wanted to prove he was good for something and wasn't just eating hay and grain that we might need for the cattle in winter. I wanted to surprise you and Ma."

"You're going to surprise her all right, but you haven't me very much. I was afraid this might happen."

He examined the gash on my head and said, "You've got a nasty little cut there. But the blood on your face makes it look worse than it is." Then he examined my foot. "It's not broken, but you've got a pretty bad sprain. I can't take you home lookin' like this. It'd scare your Ma half to death. Give me your handkerchief. I'll soak it in the creek and wash you up a little."

It only took a few minutes to go to the creek, soak his handkerchief and mine, and wash me up. "All this happened in just one try?" he asked as he worked on me.

"I tried about four times," I said.

Frank shook his head. "You're a glutton for punishment. You could have broken your neck or your arms or legs." Lucifer came near and stood watching. "I should have let Fletcher shoot you," Frank grumbled.

Soon as I was cleaned up Frank boosted me on Nellie and leading Lucifer we headed home. "This's a fine kettle of fish," he said. "Your Ma is gonna land on both of us this time like a ton of bricks. There was no excuse for this."

"I wanted to show you and Ma . . ." I began.

"You wanted to show your Ma," he cut me off. "You didn't have to show me."

I could have told him that I'd also wanted to bridge the widening gulf between Ma and me but I didn't.

At home Frank led the horses up to the porch and tied them to the post. He practically carried me into the house. Ma took one look at me and headed for the pan of water and towels. Frank went out to put the horses away.

Ellie asked immediately, "Did you get in a fight again?"

"No," I said.

I told Ma what had happened while she worked on me. She didn't say a word until Frank came in. Then she lit into both of us. "I knew something like this would happen when you came home with that useless cayuse," she said to Frank. "Fletcher knew what he was doing when he sold him to you. Whatever happened to your good sense I'll never know."

"Ma," I said, "it wasn't Frank's fault. I wanted Lucifer. He got him for me."

"I don't care about reasons. A grown man should have better sense. As for you, you almost got yourself killed trying to ride him."

"You sure did," Ellie piped up. "Gee, is your face a mess."

"Ellie," Ma snapped, "that's enough. Whatever got into you to try such a crazy stunt? Did you really think for one minute you could break that animal to ride? An outlaw that's pitched practically every good rider around?"

"He seemed so tame," I said lamely. "I was sure I could."

"There, you see," Ma said to Frank. "I want that animal sold, and sold now."

"Mabel," Frank said quietly, "nobody in the valley would buy him. You know that."

"Then give him back to Fletcher or shoot him. I won't have him around."

"Lucifer is Chris's horse," Frank said in the same quiet voice. "I'm not going to give him back to Fletcher and I won't shoot him."

"Then I will," Ma snapped. "I'll not have Christopher maimed for life."

"If Chris is maimed for life or killed you'll be as much to blame as the horse," Frank said bluntly.

Ma's head came up like a rattler about to strike.

"That pony can be broken to ride, I'm sure of it," Frank continued. "Chris rushed it today for only one reason. He wanted to prove to you the animal was good for something and wouldn't be just a liability eating hay and grain this winter that we might need for the cattle."

Ma looked at me.

"Frank told me not to ride him yet," I said. "I wanted to show you how good he was."

Some of the tightness went out of Ma's lips. Then she began winding a bandage around my head without saying a word.

Frank said, "Now I'm going to try to break this pony to ride, but I'm going to do it my way and in my own good time. Do you hear me, Chris? Then if I can't, and only then, will I think about either trying to find a buyer for him or disposing of him somehow." With that Frank picked up the milk bucket and headed for the barn.

I sat with my foot in a pan of cold water all evening. The swelling didn't seem to go down but the pain did. But I couldn't put an ounce of weight on the foot. When I finally hobbled to bed I felt about as good as anyone could who'd been tossed sky high by Lucifer four times in a row.

Everyone had turned in but Ma and she had finished

setting the table for breakfast and was about to go to bed. She stopped by me on the way to her room and said, "Christopher, I want you to know it was not just the hay Lucifer would eat that was worrying me but exactly what happened today. I was afraid you might try to ride him eventually and I'd seen what he did to other riders last year. He was a devil. The thought of you trying frightened me out of my wits." She pushed a lock of hair out of my eyes and smiled. "Remember, you're the only man I've got."

"Ma," I said, "you've got Frank." It popped out. I think I was as surprised as she was.

"We don't discuss that," she said. "Now or ever."

"But he likes you," I said.

She shook her head. "Maybe someday you'll understand." She bent and kissed me quickly and went into her room.

11

FOR SEVERAL DAYS I lay flat on my back on the bed or sat in a chair with my foot propped up. But Lucifer's bucking me off had accomplished one good thing, that void between Ma and me was gone. Her attitude toward Lucifer had changed, too. She was against him more than ever now.

Luckily Frank had finished his work for Fletcher and took over all my chores. He let Lucifer run in the corral. When I asked about him Frank said, "He's as easy to be around as any old saddle horse I've ever seen."

"That means nothing," Ma said sharply. "It's what will happen the second you try to ride him."

"I know," Frank agreed.

The third morning the bandage came off my head and that afternoon the swelling had gone down enough in my ankle to get a shoe on. I immediately hobbled out to see Lucifer.

He welcomed me with nickering and tossing his head and pushing against me like he was glad to see me. I spent an hour talking to him, petting and fussing around him. He acted like anybody could step right up and climb on his back and there'd be no trouble.

Frank came in from checking the alfalfa field and I asked, "Do you really think he can be broke to ride?"

Frank leaned on the gate and studied Lucifer. "I thought so when I got him. Now I'm not so sure."

"Why?" I asked.

"Look at him. He obviously likes you. You'd think all you had to do was climb aboard and he'd walk off like an old farm plug. But he tossed you all over that meadow. Not once. Four times. He knew exactly what he was doing. He could be a plain outlaw that's never going to be ridden. I've never been around an animal like him."

"What you're saying is that you're afraid he can't be broke to ride," I said with a sinking feeling.

Frank shook his head. "I don't know what I'm saying. I'm no horse expert. I'm hoping that maybe we just haven't yet found the proper way to approach him."

I was about to ask what would happen to Lucifer if he couldn't be ridden, then I remembered Frank's words the night he brought me home. If he couldn't break Lucifer he'd try to find a buyer or dispose of him. I knew what he meant. Shoot him.

"As soon as we get this next cutting of alfalfa in we'll really go to work on Lucifer and try to break him. The cutting's ready now. I'll mow tomorrow. Do you think you can rake in a couple of days?"

"I'm ready now," I said.

Frank mowed the next day and two days later I raked it. The foot was as good as ever. It took three days to haul the hay out of the field and stack it. Then Frank said, "Now we'll go to work on Lucifer." He drove to Fletcher's and borrowed a saddle.

"Do you really think you can ride him?" Ma asked.

"I'm no great shakes as a rider," Frank said. "But somebody's got to try if he's going to be broke."

"You be mighty careful. We don't need any broken arms and legs."

"I intend to be careful," Frank said.

The next morning after we'd finished the chores we started in. Frank went into the stall to saddle Lucifer. At sight of the saddle his ears shot forward, his head came up, and he began stamping back and forth. Frank put the saddle down. "He knows what it is." He laid the saddle blanket over Lucifer's back. The pony moved about nervously for a minute but when nothing else happened he quieted down. Frank left the blanket on a few minutes, then removed it, waited, and replaced it again. He kept doing that while I stood at his head, talked to him and petted. Finally he accepted the blanket.

Then Frank tried the saddle again. The moment its weight settled on his back he swung his head. "It's all right," I said, "easy, boy." His attention came back to me and Frank left the saddle sitting loosely without trying to cinch it up.

A few minutes later Frank carefully drew up the cinch. Lucifer didn't object. "All right," Frank said, "back him out and lead him around the corral. Keep his attention so he doesn't start thinking about what's on his back."

I did and Lucifer followed me just fine.

Ellie stuck her head between the corral rails and said, "Gee, Chris, he don't pay any attention to the saddle at all. You gonna ride him now?"

Her sudden appearance and her sharp voice startled Lucifer and he jerked his head up. "Get outa here," I hissed. "Beat it." I began talking to Lucifer and he quieted down again. When I glanced up Ellie was gone. She was standing on the porch with Ma. Ma was shading her eyes and watching us.

I said, "I'll bet I could ride him now with the saddle on."

"You've taken your lumps," Frank said. "When I figure the time's right I'll do it. Take him back to the stall now."

Frank left the saddle on for several hours so he'd get used to the feel of it and realize that just because it was there something bad wasn't going to happen to him. Then he took it off.

We repeated the performance in the afternoon.

"You think that will help?" Ma asked.

"I don't know," Frank said. "But saddling him and then piling aboard hasn't worked."

Next morning we went through the same procedure. But this time we left him tied to the snubbing post with the saddle on when we went in to lunch. Ellie asked immediately, "When you gonna ride him, Chris?"

"I'm not," I said. "Frank is."

"Right after lunch," Frank told her.

"You think he's ready now?" Ma asked.

"He's about as ready as he'll ever be. I don't see anything to be gained by waiting longer."

"That sounds a little like now or never," Ma said.

"I guess it is. He's about as tame and gentle as a horse can get. At least, that's how he acts with Chris. If he can't be ridden now he never will be."

I didn't like the sound of that. The implication scared me so bad I could hardly eat.

When we started to leave the house Ma said, "You be careful. I've seen that animal buck."

"I expect to see it very soon now," Frank said.

He didn't try right away. He fiddled with the saddle, tightened the cinch, put one foot gingerly in the stirrup and let his weight come on it. Lucifer looked around but I was at his head talking to him, petting him. We spent almost an hour fooling with him; then Frank said, "I guess this is as good a time as any. Stand clear, Chris."

I backed off as far as the water trough and then I noticed that Ma and Ellie had come down and were leaning on the corral gate watching.

Frank gathered up the reins, got hold of the horn, and carefully put a foot in the stirrup. I caught myself saying, under my breath, "Be good, Lucifer. Please, be good. Please, Lucifer."

Frank went up into the saddle in a smooth lift. That instant Lucifer exploded. His head was down between his forefeet and he shot into the air as if on springs. I've never seen anything as wild. Frank lost his hat the first jump and he whipped about on Lucifer's back like a rag. He stuck three more jumps; then he sailed into the air and landed hard on hands and knees. Lucifer stopped immediately and stood looking at him, ears cocked forward.

I ran and picked up the reins. I felt a little sick.

Ma had started through the gate to go to Frank when he got slowly to his feet and dusted off his pants. "Man, oh man!" He shook his head. "I've ridden a couple of buckers in my younger days but nothing like this hunk of dynamite."

Ma asked, "Are you all right? Are you sure you're all right?"

"I'm fine," he said, "except for my dignity." He took

the reins from my hand. "At least I know what to expect now." He stroked Lucifer's glistening shoulder. Then he took hold of the saddle horn and grinned at me, "If at first you don't succeed. . . ."

"You're not going to try again?" Ma asked.

"Mabel," he jerked his head at the saddle, "up there is the only place you can ride from. Get back outside the gate. And you back off, Chris."

He went into the saddle fast. But as fast as he was Lucifer was faster. His head was down and he was in the air, his back humped before Frank had both feet in the stirrups. He tried to bring Lucifer's head up but he didn't have a chance. He lasted about as long as he had the first time. The moment Frank left the saddle Lucifer stopped bucking as if his job were done. I picked up the reins again and held him.

Frank was slower getting up this time. Then he leaned against the snubbing post getting his breath.

Ma ran to him and took his arm. "That's enough," she said. "He'll kill you. He threw you awfully hard that time."

"I'm all right," Frank managed, "but I don't know." He smiled at Ma a little. There was a trickle of blood at the corner of his mouth. "Maybe you're right and he can't be ridden."

I said fearfully, "You're not going to quit? You're not giving up?"

"Let's say I'm beginning to have a few healthy doubts."

Ma was looking at Lucifer nibbling thoughtfully at the tip of her finger. "Maybe you aren't going about this the right way."

"To break a horse somebody's got to ride him," Frank

pointed out. "And that's where I seem to be having a bit of trouble."

"That's what I mean," Ma said. "I watched each time you started to get on. He was ready and waiting for you. His mind was made up to buck and he started immediately before you were firmly settled in the saddle. You didn't get a chance to pull his head up. A horse can't buck until he gets his head down."

"Where did you get all this horse knowledge?" Frank asked.

"I told you I was raised on a farm in the East. My father was very good with horses. He probably broke half the horses in our county. It was his way of earning extra money. I've heard him talk about horses many times and the things he did to a particularly bad one."

"What do you suppose he'd have done with this one?"

"Father always said a horse had a one-track mind. Lucifer knows you're going to try to ride him and he's just waiting for you to make your move, then he beats you to it."

"He does that all right. How would you suggest I take his mind off tossing me sky high?"

"Give him something else to think about."

"Like what? He's pretty set on dumping me."

Ma nibbled thoughtfully at the tip of her finger. "You might try dropping a pebble in his ear."

"You mean a rock! You're joking."

"Father broke a horse like this once. That's what he did. Of course the pebble has to be big enough so it won't go down far into the ear, only into the outer ear," Ma explained. "You have to time it just right and drop the pebble at the moment you mount. He immediately begins tossing his head to get rid of it. It takes his mind off anything else. By the time he has the pebble out you should be well set in the saddle and ready for him."

"That's pretty farfetched."

"It worked for Father. You're not getting anywhere the way you're going at it now."

"All right," Frank agreed. "I can't take many more spills like these. Chris, find me a rock about an inch or so in diameter."

I found two. He took one and said, "Keep the other for an emergency." Then Ma and I stepped back and let Frank go at it.

He gathered up the reins and Lucifer stood quietly, waiting, ears back, head turned slightly watching Frank. The last moment Frank dropped the stone into his ear and in the same motion vaulted into the saddle.

Lucifer began shaking and jerking his head like mad trying to get rid of the stone. In a few seconds it popped out. Frank was ready for him. Those big hands had the pony's head up and no matter how he tried he couldn't get it down. They fought all over the corral raising a dust cloud but Frank kept his head high. Lucifer was streaked with sweat and clearly tired when he finally stopped, at a loss for what to do.

Frank said, "Open the gate."

Ma swung the gate wide. Lucifer danced through and they went out across the pasture, the pony fighting Frank all the way. They were gone about twenty minutes. When they returned Lucifer was still trying to get his head down to buck. But it didn't seem to me he was fighting quite as hard as before. Frank stepped down and handed me the reins. "I think you're going to have a working horse here,

Chris," he smiled. "But he's not ready for you to ride yet."

"Ma," I said excitedly, "you hear that? He's going to be worth something."

Ma studied Lucifer critically, arms folded. By her expression I couldn't tell if she was pleased, displeased, or what. "I think you're right," she said. Then she turned and went to the house.

We took the saddle off, I rubbed Lucifer down, gave him a big feed of oats, and curried and brushed and talked to him. In a half hour or so he quieted down.

Frank rode him again later that day and used the pebble again. It went as it had before. Lucifer gave him a battle. But it didn't last as long as the morning one had.

Frank rode him again the next day, then he let me try it. I purposely went right up to the porch and yelled for Ma. She and Ellie came out.

Ellie said, "Gee, you ain't scared he'll throw you?"

" 'Course not," I said. "He's just like riding Nellie now. Only more fun." Lucifer snorted delicately. He tossed his head and stamped his feet. His sharp ears jumped back and forth. "See, Ma," I said, "he's a working horse now."

"Maybe," Ma said thoughtfully. "He looks pretty fractious to me."

"It's just his way. He's full of life."

"I don't trust him," Ma said in a positive voice. "You be mighty careful." I knew then there was no convincing her. She didn't like Lucifer and nothing was going to change her.

That afternoon Frank took the saddle back to Fletcher's.

In the following weeks, before school started, I rode everywhere bareback. I even went into town. Sheriff Ed

Peck and Mr. Wright came out of the store to look at Lucifer. The Sheriff said, "You've got a might nice lookin' pony there. That couldn't be Sam Fletcher's black bucker, could it?"

"He was," I said so proud I was ready to bust. "He's mine now."

"And you're ridin' him." The Sheriff smiled at me. "You're quite a buckeroo as well as fighter."

"Frank broke him," I said.

Mr. Wright adjusted his gold-rimmed glasses and peered close at Lucifer. "A boy ridin' Sam Fletcher's bucker. I swan to man I wouldn't have believed it. Well! Well!"

I went into the store to get some groceries Ma wanted and while Mr. Wright was filling the order I slipped down to the gun department. The little single-shot .22 rifle was still there.

Lucifer never did really quiet down and plug along like Nellie. His head was always high, his ears jumping back and forth, his nostrils flared, and he snorted delicately as he pranced along looking like he was about to bust loose any second. I loved all that but Ma didn't, so her distrust continued.

The morning school started Ma wouldn't let us ride Lucifer double. So Ellie rode Nellie. "You stay with Ellie," Ma cautioned me, "and don't let that black Satan get Nellie excited." We poked along side by side. Nellie, head down, taking her time, Lucifer dancing and acting like he wanted to take off into a headlong run.

That fall I was in the eighth grade.

12

LUCIFER made me one of the most important kids in school that fall. Of course, being in eighth grade helped. But mostly it was Lucifer. Everybody knew Sam Fletcher's Fourth of July bucking horse that no one in the valley had been able to ride. And here I had him and was riding him to school every day. Some of the other kids might have been able to ride him now, but nobody tried. He cut quite a figure with that gleaming black coat and his mincing, dancing, head-high strut and I enjoyed every second of the attention the sight of him brought me.

As far as Ma was concerned Lucifer was still impractical. When I bragged about how he behaved and how I liked riding him her remarks were always short and noncommittal. Like the time I met Mr. Fletcher on the road and he said, "Boy, if I'd known that horse could be broke to ride like you're doin' I'd never sold him. Frank got a mighty good buy off me."

I repeated, "He said Frank got a mighty good buy, Ma."

"I heard you," she said in that tone which closed the conversation.

I still felt we were more like boarders or something in Frank's house. When Frank was in, Ma carefully kept to her own side. Frank stayed pretty much to his. Ellie and I paid no attention to that invisible split. But I'd given up all hope that we'd ever become a real family.

First frost dusted the roofs and the tops of the rail fences. The potato vines turned black. I spent the weekend digging potatoes and storing them in the root cellar, a hole in the ground with a sod roof. We also stored the carrots, onions, turnips, and beets there.

The leaves of the cottonwoods along the creek turned brown and fell, leaving the trees with bare limbs thrust up against graying skies. The alfalfa stopped growing. The wild grass turned yellow and brittle. Now the wind coming off Christmas Ridge had a bite. We began to feed our cattle a small amount of hay from the stacks in the field. From now on there was little ranch work to do. I was free to come and go as I liked on weekends.

Lucifer and I explored far and wide. We followed the creek for miles, cut across ridges, and dropped into small valleys I never dreamed existed. We kicked jack rabbits and pheasants out from under our feet. We saw the first migrating ducks and geese stop to rest along the creek on their way south. Any number of times we jumped coyotes and deer and watched them dash off across the land. I mentioned to Ma that if I had a little .22 single-shot rifle like the one in Wright's gun rack in town I could keep us well supplied with wild game.

"Guns and ammunition cost money," Ma said.

"It'd pay for itself," I pointed out. "We wouldn't have to eat any of our own beef."

"You've got a point," Frank smiled.

"But not enough of a point," Ma said, and went on to something else that was bothering her. "You be mighty careful you don't get lost with all this galavanting around. We wouldn't know where to start looking for you."

"You don't have to worry about that," Frank said. "If Chris got lost Lucifer knows the way home."

"You think that pony knows anything besides prancing down the road acting smart?"

"You know he does, if you know as much about horses as you seem to."

Ma said nothing.

About the middle of November the first snow storm boiled down off Christmas Ridge. For a few hours we could hardly see the barn from the house. Then it quit. Two days later you wouldn't have known it snowed. We all breathed easier.

Near the middle of December we went to town one Saturday morning. Ma, Ellie, and Frank went in the wagon. I rode Lucifer. The night before Ma told Ellie and me, "Christmas will soon be here so tomorrow you can both shop at Wright's for a present. You can each have one. But don't pick the most expensive thing. We can't afford to spend much."

I knew exactly what I wanted. I walked straight through the store to the gun rack. The little .22 single-shot was still there. I pointed to it and said, "I want that."

"A rifle," Ma said.

"A .22 rifle," I corrected her.

Frank said, "A boy, a horse, and a gun. That figures."

Mr. Wright said, "You've been watching that gun a long time, haven't you, son?"

"Yes, sir, I have."

Ma was nibbling at the point of a finger thoughtfully and frowning at me. "A rifle. But you're only going on thirteen, Christopher."

"I had my first when I was eleven," Frank said.

"A rifle can kill. Christopher doesn't know a thing about handling a gun."

"He will when I finish training him. The only thing he'll kill will be what he aims at. How much is that rifle, Mr. Wright?"

"Seeing as Chris, here, helped you in the fight last summer and I haven't been able to move it—to him it's seven dollars. That's about what I paid for it."

"I don't know." Ma was still nibbling at her finger.

"It would pay for itself in no time," I said. "Besides keeping us in fresh meat I might get a coyote or two and the bounty would pay for the gun. Ma, it's really practical."

Frank burst out laughing. "Now, there's an argument you can't beat. Besides, every man in this country should be familiar with firearms. Chris is a couple of years overdue learning. For a Christmas present I think he's kept the expense pretty reasonable."

"Well," Ma conceded, "all right. But you don't get the gun until Christmas eve."

I had my present, the little .22 and two boxes of shells.

We went to look for Ellie. She was on the far side of the store, right in the middle of counters stacked with tops, wind-up trains, clowns, Christmas tinsel, and I don't know what all. One look and we all knew that she'd found what she wanted. It was a stuffed toy about eighteen inches tall and looked a lot like a cute, cuddly bear cub. It was brown and it had button eyes and a button nose and was covered with some kind of cloth that looked a little like fur. Ellie stood in front of it smiling, her eyes shining. She looked at Ma and Frank. She didn't say a word.

"What on earth is that thing?" Ma asked.

"That's known as a teddy bear," Mr. Wright said. "I understand it was named in honor of President Theodore Roosevelt. He's a great hunter, you know. This is the first year we'd had them. They're a very good seller."

Ma asked, "Is that what you want? You're sure?" When Ellie nodded Ma turned up the price tag and looked at it. She bit her lip and said quietly to Frank, "This is almost as much as Christopher's gun. And the gun, at least, is practical." She said to Ellie again, "Are you sure that's what you want? Have you looked at everything else?"

Ellie didn't take her eyes from the teddy bear. "I want it," she said in a small, positive voice.

Frank said, "Christmas comes but once a year and she'll never be seven again." He picked up the teddy bear and handed it to Ellie. She held it close, put her cheek against its face, and rocked back and forth, her eyes shut, smiling ecstatically.

Mr. Wright said, "Oh, I'm sorry. That one's sold. Mrs. Myers bought it. She's coming back within the hour to pick it up."

Ellie clutched the teddy bear to her and began to cry. She didn't cry often, but when she did she could really whoop it up. Tears poured down her cheeks and she sobbed, "I want it. I want it."

"Can you get another?" Frank asked.

"Of course," Mr. Wright said. "I'll order it out from the wholesaler. It'll take a week or so."

"Can it be here by Christmas?" Ma asked.

"It can be here."

"Order us one. Just like this," Frank said.

"There, you see, honey," Ma said, "you're going to get your teddy bear. Not this one, but another one just like it. Yours will be here for Christmas, too. Now give this one to Mr. Wright."

Ellie wiped her eyes and reluctantly gave the toy back. A few minutes later we left town. Our Christmas shopping was over. I cut a small juniper, moved limbs from one side to the other to even it up and it made a good Christmas tree. We decorated it with paper chains, popcorn strings, and popcorn balls that we made sitting around the table at night. My gun, carefully wrapped, and the two boxes of shells were put under the tree. Almost every day Ellie asked Frank when he was going in to town to get her teddy bear. Each time he explained patiently that it wasn't time yet.

"You're sure it'll come?"

"I'm sure, Baby. Don't worry, it'll be here in time."

It was the twentieth of December when Frank drove in to get the teddy bear. It hadn't come. Ellie threw a howling fit when he returned home. Frank finally quieted her only after he'd explained several times that Mr. Wright had assured him it would surely arrive with the next shipment which was due two days before Christmas.

Then Ellie came down with her first bout of winter sore throat. Ma thought her disappointment over the teddy bear and a downturn in the weather brought it on. She wouldn't let her go to school.

For the next several days Ma dosed her up with all the usual remedies but they didn't seem to help. The third night when I got home from school even I could see Ellie was worse. She wasn't eating, or couldn't, and she didn't sleep. Like Lucifer her mind was set in one track. That darned teddy bear. She kept asking in a plaintive little voice when Frank was going after it. It did no good to explain he was going in tomorrow. Ten minutes later she was asking again. Ma finally concluded that she had to be a little delirious. During the night I heard Ma up with her, putting hot cloths around her neck, wiping her face and forehead with cold water, coaxing her to swallow something, trying to get her to sleep.

Ellie was no better in the morning and neither was the weather. Ma didn't look very good either, having been up most of the night. Ellie just lay in bed looking very small, her cheeks flushed and her eyes too bright. Tomorrow night would be Christmas eve. It didn't look very promising for a merry one.

We were sitting down to breakfast when Frank said to Ma, "Could Chris miss a day of school? There's a blizzard making sure and I'd like to drive the cattle down into the timber along the creek for protection. It'll take two of us."

"Of course." Ma sat down and pushed the hair tiredly from her face. "Can we get that teddy bear somehow today? She keeps asking for it."

"You think it might help somehow?" Frank asked.

"I don't know. I've tried everything else. It's the only thing she has on her mind. Maybe if she had it she'd get some sleep."

"It won't come in until late this afternoon," Frank said. "If we don't have a raging blizzard and a foot of snow by then I'll ride in for it."

I piled on all the winter clothes I had and they were none too much. The wind swirling across the flat land off Christmas Ridge cut like a knife. The leaden sky held every promise of snow.

The cattle were bunched up against the lee of a small hill trying to keep warm. We had trouble getting them started and it took several hours to work them down into the low land and timber bordering the creek. There it was almost calm and compared to the open flat land at least ten degrees warmer. If the storm lasted any time it would be easy to bring hay down here to them.

The first driving snow shower hit us before we got home and the air was so cold the snow didn't melt. It was past noon when we rode into the barn.

The first thing we both asked Ma was, "How's Ellie?"

Ma shook her head. "I see no change."

"Soon as I have a bite I'll go into town and get the teddy bear before the storm hits."

I said, "Let me go. I'm about seventy pounds lighter. I can make it faster. It'll be easier on Lucifer."

Frank looked at Ma.

"All right," she said.

I swallowed a cup of hot cocoa and a sandwich and ran out to get Lucifer.

Even the short time I'd been in the house it had gotten colder. It was spitting a little snow again. The wind had picked up.

It wasn't too bad going in to town because the wind was at my back. It was past the middle of the afternoon when I got there. Snow was coming down steadily driven by a cutting wind.

The mail hadn't come in. It arrived every other day by

wagon or buggy from the rail head about five miles away. I wandered around the store and waited.

An hour passed. It was snowing much harder. I could barely see across the street and the driving wind was building drifts against the buildings' fronts. The street was empty. Mr. Wright stepped outside every few minutes to look for the mail wagon. "Getting mighty cold," he said once and added wood to the pot-bellied stove. I could feel the cold seeping through the walls. Mr. Wright and I stayed close to the vicinity of the stove.

Lucifer stood humped, head down at the hitch rail. There was a solid sheet of snow across his back. I went out and brushed it off and patted him. Mr. Wright came to the door and tossed me a blanket. I draped it over Lucifer's back.

It was almost dark when the mail wagon pulled up in front and Jess Miller came in dragging a pair of mail sacks. "Train was late," he explained, "and I couldn't make no time comin' back. This's a humdinger of a blizzard. Looks like the thermometer's gonna punch right out the bottom."

The teddy bear was there. Mr. Wright put it in a gunny sack for me to make it easier carrying. He said, "Are you sure you can make it home all right? You're welcome to stay here with Mrs. Wright and me till this blows over."

"I'll be fine," I said.

"If you find it too bad come back," he called as I went out the door.

It was much worse than I thought it would be. I was facing right into it and the wind blew the heat right out of my body. The driving snow was so thick I could see but a few feet and the force of it stung my face and almost blinded me. For once even Lucifer plodded along with his head down. The snow was already so deep I was guessing where the road was. I tried to keep track of my progress by familiar spots. But I only recognized a few, like some big rock beside the road, a certain tree, a sharp turn. I knew when I passed the place where Pa and Frank had their fight. There was the bank on the left, the drop-off on the right.

Then I was out on the flat valley floor and the wind hit me full blast. I considered turning back and staying with the Wrights. Then I thought of Ellie and knew I had to go on. I hunched over Lucifer as much as I could to break the wind, held the sack with the teddy bear in one hand and the reins in the other. There was no use trying to see ahead in this blinding snow, so I looked down at Lucifer's bobbing neck. I patted him and mumbled, "You're doing fine. Just fine." But I knew he didn't hear me.

I wasn't even sure I was on the road any more until I almost ran into the big juniper. We'd passed it a few feet when I remembered something Frank had said and stopped. The day last summer when we'd climbed to the top of Christmas Ridge together and he saw the road makes a big almost half circle getting to our place. He said, "Man on horseback could save about a mile if he left the road at just about that big juniper and cut across country."

In this cold and the slow pace we were traveling that mile looked awfully big. All I had to do was turn left off the road, travel straight ahead and I'd get home sooner. The wind would no longer be hitting me in the face. I'd be at right angles to it with it driving against my right side, which would help keep me warmer. Just keep that storm hitting your right side and you'll be traveling in a straight line, I told myself.

I turned Lucifer and headed away from the road. I immediately felt a little warmer and even Lucifer perked up a little. But now I was traveling across strange country with no familiar landmarks to measure my progress. I tried to gauge my time, the distance I'd come, but I soon realized that was impossible.

It seemed like I traveled a long time hunched down inside my coat. A kind of numbness came over me and I just sat there. Then I began to think I should be getting near home. I tried to fight myself into alertness by shaking my head and rubbing a mitten across my face. The house, the barn, should be coming out of this white wall at me any minute. At least I should hit a fence I could follow or something familiar.

The driving push of the storm kept clawing at me. I felt drowsy and dull. I remembered that I'd heard this was the first indication of freezing. That frightened me into becoming more alert. I considered getting off and walking to restore circulation. But if I did I wouldn't be able to get on again. Sometime later I became aware that something had changed. I stopped Lucifer and tried to reason it out. Then I knew. The wind was no longer hitting me on the right side. It was almost at my back. Had the wind shifted or were we heading in another direction? Had I unconsciously turned Lucifer to get away from the wind, or had he done it? Had whatever happened just taken place or was it some minutes ago? I decided to retrace my tracks to see if I'd turned.

Within a couple of hundred feet the tracks were filled in with blowing snow. I stopped and looked about completely awake now. In the few feet I could see there was nothing familiar, nothing to give me a clue as to which direction I'd been heading or was headed now. I put the storm on my right side again. Then I sat there. I'd been traveling with the storm almost at my back for some time. So even if I was now headed in the right direction I was so far off course I could miss the house as much as half a mile or even a mile. That could be fatal. I was confused. In this freezing, savage storm I was utterly lost.

For a minute I almost panicked and whipped Lucifer up to drive him straight into the storm and ride and ride. All I could think was that I was going to freeze to death. I remembered stories of people getting lost between the house and barn and freezing to death. Then I got hold of myself. The only way I'd get out of this alive was to keep my head. I had probably the best horse in the valley under me. Frank had said that if I got lost wandering around Lucifer would bring me home. Cats and dogs and horses had that homing instinct. But if I let Lucifer have his head could he find his way in this storm? And would he go to our place or back to his old home at Fletcher's? It didn't matter, I decided, just so he got someplace where there was shelter.

I tied the reins around his neck, then lay down flat along his back to get all the warmth I could from his body, put my arms around his neck, and said, "It's up to you, Lucifer. Let's go. Take us home, boy."

Lucifer turned partially into the wind and started off as if he knew exactly where he was going.

I lost all track of time. I began to wonder if I was beginning to freeze because I didn't seem quite so cold, or was the heat from the pony's body getting through to me. I was conscious of the constant rhythm of his walking, the cut of the wind and the endless driving snow. Sometimes I lifted my head to try to spot something familiar. I recognized nothing. I passed brush clumps almost buried by drifting snow, crossed several shallow gullies, and once skirted a low hill. They were all strange. Finally I put my head down, shut my eyes, and gave myself completely into Lucifer's keeping. He plodded straight ahead never faltering. How long we traveled that way I don't know. I began to wonder, vaguely, if he, too, was wandering in a circle, lost. Then I was aware he'd stopped. I raised my head and we were right in front of the barn.

I slid off and fell in the snow. I was trying to get to my feet when powerful hands lifted me and there was Frank. He carried me up to the house, set me down in his chair, and said to Ma, "Get these clothes off him. He's half frozen. I'll be right back."

Ma pulled the chair close to the roaring stove and began peeling clothes off me. I was so cold that at first I couldn't feel the heat.

Ma had me wrapped in blankets when Frank returned. He began rubbing my arms and legs to restore circulation. It felt like he was rubbing the skin right off. Ma made me a steaming cup of cocoa and I gulped it down. Gradually I began to get warm. "How's Lucifer?" I asked.

"He's all right," Frank said. "I gave him a big feed of oats and some hay. What happened that took you so long?"

"The mail was late. Then I tried to take that short cut that starts at the big juniper and I got lost. Lucifer brought me home." I looked straight at Ma and said, "He saved my life. Nellie would never have made it home."

Ma nodded, then she picked up the teddy bear and disappeared into the bedroom.

"I guessed about the mail," Frank said, "and I debated

whether to head out and try to find you or to wait. I figured you'd stick with the road, but that if you did somehow become lost you'd have sense enough to give Lucifer his head and he'd bring you home. I was getting ready to head out to try to find you when you came in."

Ma returned and I asked, "How's Ellie?"

"It's not Christmas eve but I gave her the teddy bear. She's not asleep but—well, come take a look if you feel like walking that far."

Ellie had the teddy bear clasped tight in her arms. Her eyes were shut but she was smiling.

IT WAS one of those typical early winter storms. Wind howled around the corners of the house most of the night. When I awoke in the morning it had blown itself out and our white world was utterly still and peaceful. We had about eight inches of snow on the level but against the barn and house it had piled up as much as three feet. Frank said the temperature was rising fast and the cattle down among the trees along the creek wouldn't even have to be fed.

Ellie was better. At least her cheeks weren't flushed, her eyes didn't have that glassy stare, and she'd got some sleep. She came out to breakfast carrying the teddy bear. She didn't eat anything, her throat being so sore and swollen, but she drank some hot milk then she returned to bed carrying the bear. I decided this would be a pretty good Christmas eve after all.

I finished breakfast as fast as I could and ran out to see Lucifer. Frank followed behind with the milk pail.

Lucifer was standing in his stall, head down, back humped, and his legs spread apart as if he were bracing himself from falling. His mouth was open and I could hear his labored breathing before I got to the stall. Most of his oats were still in the grain box and he hadn't touched the hay. I went into the stall and began to pet him and talk to him. He kept his head down and that wheezing, panting sound, as if he were fighting for air, went on. His black coat glistened with sweat.

Frank came into the barn and I yelled, "Frank, come look at Lucifer."

Frank put the milk pail down and walked around the pony scowling. He ran a hand over his sweating coat and down his front legs. He felt of his ears, looked at his eyes, and listened to his labored breathing.

I asked, fearfully, "What's wrong with him, Frank? He's sick, isn't he?"

Frank nodded. "He's sick all right. He's mighty sick. I should have come out and checked him during the night. But I didn't dream of anything like this. His legs and ears are cold and he's having a lot of trouble breathing. And this sweating."

"What is it?" I asked. "What's wrong?"

"I saw these symptoms once before, a long time ago. I'd say Lucifer's got frosted lungs, or pneumonia. Don't know which, or maybe they're the same."

"What caused it?"

"That ride you made last night in the blizzard."

"What can we do?" I was suddenly frantic with fear. "We've got to help him. We've got to."

"We'll do all we can," Frank said quietly. "Just don't get all excited. That won't help."

"I don't want anything to happen to him. What can we do?"

"First off get some sacks and rub him down good. Get this sweat off him so he won't get any colder. After you've rubbed him down with the sacks rub him down again with hay, especially his legs, they're cold. The hay is rough. It'll help stimulate his circulation. While you're doing that I'll do the milking."

I worked hard and fast. By the time I'd finished rubbing Lucifer down Frank was through milking and turned Fawn out. We went to the house together. The minute I got inside I burst out, "Ma, Lucifer's sick."

Ma looked at Frank. "What's wrong with him?"

Frank explained and said, "Have you got some blankets we can use to put over him to get him warm?"

"All our blankets are on the bed," Ma said.

"He can have mine." I went to my bed, scooped them up, and walked out. Ma's lips were suddenly tight but she let me go.

We draped the blankets over Lucifer's back and tied them around his body with twine. We both rubbed and rubbed on his legs to start the circulation and get them warm. Then we wrapped them with sacks and tied these with twine. Frank brought in a bucket of fresh water and tried to get him to drink. It was no use. We tried him with fresh hay and oats. He just stood there, head down, not interested in anything.

There was an area about twenty feet square between the stalls and where the hay was stored. We spread it deep with straw and put Lucifer in there where we had more room to work around him. He could barely walk those few feet. There he stood spread-legged, head down, that rasping breathing going on and on.

"He's going to be all right, isn't he?" I asked fearfully. "He won't die, Frank?"

Frank said, "Chris, I'm not a veterinarian. I don't know much about horses' sicknesses. Like most ranchers I know how to work 'em, and I've got a few home remedies when they get sick. I hope he's going to be all right. We're going to do everything we possibly can for him. I can't promise you any more."

"Isn't there a horse doctor, a veterinarian, we can get some place?"

Frank shook his head. "Not within a hundred miles that I know of."

"What do other ranchers do when their horses get sick?"

"The same thing we're doing. Then nature either gets them well or they die. Frosted lung isn't necessarily fatal and Lucifer has several things going for him. He's young and he's always been strong and healthy."

We stayed with Lucifer all forenoon. He moved around a little. Mostly he stood in one place, head down, legs braced, and panting. He wouldn't eat or drink. He seemed very weak and unsteady. About noon he lay down. He couldn't get up again.

We left him there and went in to lunch. But I couldn't eat. I finally went back out to him.

He hadn't moved. He lay on his side, his sack-wrapped legs stretched out like sticks, his head lying flat on the straw. I felt under the blanket. His body was warm. His legs were warm. I tried to tempt him with hay, then a handful of oats. He paid no attention. I sat down at his head and began to stroke him. "You've got to eat," I said. "You've got to eat or you'll die. Please eat, Lucifer. Don't die. Please, don't die." I started to cry. I sat there petting him and crying.

I don't know when Frank and Ma came in. But there they were. I turned my head away and wiped my eyes so they wouldn't see the tears.

"Christopher," Ma said, "don't take it so hard. It's not as if he was a really valuable horse."

That did it! I was on my feet facing her and all my frustrations, fears, and disappointments came pouring out. I wasn't only mad at what she'd said, but the way she'd continued to act the past months. It flooded out like a dam breaking. I was half crying, half shouting at her.

"You would say that! You've hated him from the day he came. You weren't even willing to give him a chance. And you wouldn't have given him any credit no matter what he did. To you he was bad from the very beginning. He could never do anything right. You never tried to understand or make allowances. Well, he saved my life last night. And maybe he did Ellie some good bringing that silly bear home for her. That don't mean a thing to you. But it does to me. I'm going to try to save him if it's the last thing I ever do, whether you like it or not."

Ma looked at me like she couldn't believe what she'd heard. "That was a very stupid thing for me to say," she said softly. "I didn't mean it the way it sounded. I'm sorry."

"You're not sorry for anything you say!" I raged. "You always mean what you say. You make up your mind and you never change it. Never! No matter what. You've never given an inch in your whole life. You never will."

I was out of breath and run down. I turned my back on Ma and sat down again at Lucifer's head. I was shaking inside and blinded by tears.

For a moment it was deathly still in the barn. Then Frank said quietly, "We've got to turn him over, Chris. If he lies in this position too long he'll get twisted gut and that'll be the end of him. Take hold of his front legs. I'll take the back."

We rolled Lucifer over easily and he just sort of sighed. We covered him up again.

Ma watched, arms folded. She didn't say a word until we had him covered. Then she said, "Christopher, I'd like to help." Her voice sounded very small and kind of plaintive, like Ellie's when her throat was sore and she went to Ma for help.

Frank said, "Mabel, we'll take any kind of help. And glad to get it. What do you suggest?"

"That breathing sounds like penumonia," Ma said. "Why don't you doctor him like you would a human?"

"I've never doctored a human with pneumonia."

"I have. Christopher, go fill some kettles and pails with water, put them on the stove and build up a roaring fire. I want lots of hot water. Then bring the tub out here."

"What're you going to do?" Frank asked.

"I'm going to put a mustard plaster on his chest for one thing."

I left the barn without a word.

While I filled kettles with water, put them on the stove, and built up a roaring fire, Ma was mixing a bowl of yellow mustard and water. We were ready about the same time. I carried the tub and a half-dozen newspapers. Ma had the bowl of mustard and a blanket she'd taken from Frank's bed.

Ma sat down in the straw beside Lucifer, shoved back the blanket, and began to spread the mustard over his chest, back, and sides with a knife. "Here's where the trouble is," she explained. "This area needs lots of heat and this will make it." When she finished she put the newspapers over the mustard and the blanket over that. "We'll leave this on a few hours."

She rose and stood looking down at Lucifer. "He's awfully weak. He's got to eat." She frowned, nibbling thoughtfully at a finger. "I'm going to try something. I give Ellie milk with an egg in it when her sore throat's so bad she can't swallow solid food." She turned and left the barn.

I began to feel better. Ma had taken over and she went about it bustling with purpose. She'd doctored Ellie and me through all sorts of sicknesses. She'd do the same for Lucifer.

She was back in minutes with a gallon of milk into which she'd beaten a half-dozen eggs. Frank held up Lucifer's head. Ma held the milk under his nose and began to talk to him just as she did with Ellie and me when we were sick. "Come on, Lucifer," she coaxed. "This's good. Just taste it. Doesn't it smell good. Taste it, Lucifer. Just taste it." She dipped a palmful and smeared it on his mouth. He pulled his head away.

Ma stood up after a minute and Frank let Lucifer's head down. "He won't drink milk, at least not now. So we'll have to wait." She felt under the blanket. "The mustard's making him warm. That's good."

Frank and Ma sat down in the hay to wait and watch. Ma sent me to the house to check the stove and Ellie. Ellie was sitting in a chair rocking the teddy bear. I thought she looked better. She asked, "Is Lucifer all right?"

"No," I said.

"Is he going to die, Chris?"

"I don't know," I mumbled. I filled the stove and brought in two big armloads of wood. The water in the pails and pans covering the stove top was barely warm. Ellie went back to bed.

When I returned to the barn I noticed water dripping steadily from the eaves. It was thawing.

Ma said, "We heard it dripping a few minutes ago."

Lucifer lay as he had. "Will the weather getting warmer help?" I asked.

"I always like to think so," Ma said. "Certainly he shouldn't chill so easily. You might open the door and let in more fresh air. Fresh air is important."

I opened the door part way, then sat down at Lucifer's head and gently stroked his face and listened to the steady drip of melting snow.

We turned Lucifer again. He sort of groaned and sighed, but he made no effort to rise. Ma felt about under the blanket then ran her hand down his legs. "He seems warm." She tried him again with the bucket of milk. It was no use. "Christopher," she said, "go to the root cellar and get a half-dozen of big, juicy carrots. We've got to tempt his appetite somehow."

I ran for the carrots. Lucifer refused them. Ma pried his jaws apart and put a carrot in his mouth. He spit it out. "Well," she murmured, "that didn't work."

We waited again.

Ma went to the house to check on Ellie but soon returned.

Frank cleaned Jess and Gyp's stables, put fresh hay in the mangers, and came back.

I went to the house twice and stoked the stove. The last time I filled the woodbox again. The kettles of water were steaming. Ellie was asleep, the teddy bear tight in her arms. When I returned to the barn first dusk was creeping across the snow. The thawing drips had now become small streams running off the roof. I took off my mackinaw. It would soon be Christmas eve.

There was no change in Lucifer.

Ma asked, "How long has the mustard plaster been on?"

Frank looked at his watch, "Almost five hours."

"Let's take it off and try the hot packs. They always seem to help Ellie more than anything else. We'll have to wash off the mustard. Christopher, fill the tub about half full of hot water. Then refill the buckets and put them on the stove again."

It didn't take long to wash off the mustard. Then Ma soaked the blanket she'd taken from Frank's bed and wrung it out. They draped it around and under Lucifer's chest then packed dry gunny sacks against it to hold it in place. "That's making a lot more heat than the mustard plaster," Ma said. "After supper we'll change it again."

Supper was a quick pick-up meal that we ate hurriedly. Ellie ate a little for the first time, then went back to bed. I didn't eat much. I hadn't the heart for it. I was about to leave for the barn again when Ma went to the Christmas tree and got the package with the .22 rifle in it and laid it in my lap. "Merry Christmas, Christopher," she said.

I sat there and held it, I didn't even feel like unwrapping it. Here I had the gun I'd wanted for months and it didn't mean a thing to me. All I could think of was Lucifer lying out in the barn and probably dying. I managed to mumble, "Thanks, thanks a lot." Then I laid the gun down on the table and went out. It was the worst Christmas eve I've ever known.

As soon as Ma and Frank came to the barn they changed the blanket on Lucifer again. After that they changed it about every half-hour or so when the blanket got cool. It kept me humping to keep them in hot water.

The stars came out in a cloudless sky and Christmas Ridge rose sheer and white in the moonlight. Water ran steadily from the eaves. Frank lit the lantern and hung it from a nail. I milked Fawn, strained the milk, and put it in pans for the cream to rise. Then it was time to change the blanket on Lucifer again and I ran for hot water. Changing the blanket, turning him, trying to coax him to eat, to drink. That went on for hours.

It must have been somewhere near midnight when Lucifer stirred, lifted his head briefly, and dropped it again. Ma bent over him. She ran her hands under the blanket, moving them over his chest and legs. "He feels plenty warm," she said. She looked closely at his eyes. "They seem a little clearer. I wonder . . ." She left the words hanging there.

"Could be some kind of reflex action," Frank said.

"Maybe." Ma's voice had a note of excitement. "Christopher, get at his head and take hold of the halter. Frank"—it was the first time in all the months we'd been there that she didn't say "Mr. Chase" when we were alone—"take his tail. We're going to try to get him up. We've simply got to get him on his feet or he's never going to make it."

I pulled and Frank lifted and we all talked and coaxed him. Lucifer groaned and partially sat up, then he collapsed back on his side.

Ma tried the milk again. It was no use. She tried the

carrot. His nostrils fluttered, his lips moved. But he didn't take it.

"It's no use, Mabel," Frank said gently. "We tried. We've done everything we can think of and he's worse than when we found him this morning. He's too weak to stand even if we could get him up. He knows it, too."

"You mean he's going to die?" I asked.

"Not die," Frank said. "There's no sense letting him suffer. When there's no hope you put an animal out of its misery."

"Shoot him! No! No! You can't do that. You can't!" I looked at Ma as I always did when I was in trouble.

She was looking down at Lucifer thoughtfully nibbling at the end of her finger. Then I saw her chin come up and her back straighten. I knew she'd made up her mind about something. She had that indomitable, stubborn look about her that I'd seen the morning we'd walked into Frank Chase's cabin and she announced that we'd come to stay. It was something wonderful and strong and unbeatable. My sagging spirits were immediately uplifted. "I'm not licked," she said in that positive voice. "I will not quit." She looked at Frank. "Do you have any whiskey?"

"Whiskey? You mean for a stimulant? Something to give him a boost?"

"Exactly."

Frank shook his head. "There's no whiskey around here. Never has been. And I don't know how you'd get it tonight of all nights."

Ma was still nibbling at her finger. "Harry brought home a bottle a couple of times. He didn't know I found out. He used to keep it in the grain bin in the barn. I wonder if there could be one there now."

I said, "I'll ride over on Nellie and see."

"You're not afraid at night?"

"Nothing to be afraid of," I said. "It's thawing and it's moonlight."

It was a beautiful night. The moonlight on the snow made it almost as bright as day, just the kind of night Christmas eve should be.

Our old place was dark and quiet. I left the barn door open and the moonlight flooded in and lit the interior. I went straight to the grain bin, threw up the lid, and felt around inside. There was a bottle. I lifted it out and held it up to the light. It was empty. In the hope that Pa had stashed another somewhere I hunted around on beams and ledges. There was nothing.

14

I WENT OUTSIDE and stood looking up at Christmas Ridge rising sheer and white into the night blue. The hope that had built up in me at Ma's fighting stand was beginning to leak away. I felt that getting this liquor was a sort of last-ditch stand for her. I just had to find some. I considered riding into town and waking the owner of the Pastime. But I didn't know where he lived or if he'd be home on this night. Running Nellie into town and back would take a good three hours. She wasn't as fast or strong as Lucifer. The next couple of hours could be critical for Lucifer.

Then I thought of Sam Fletcher. His place was just over Christmas Ridge, a half-hour's ride away. If he didn't have liquor some of his dozen riders certainly would. This was Christmas eve and they'd probably be celebrating.

Sam Fletcher's house was dark, so were the bunkhouse

windows. I pounded on the house door and kept pounding. Finally there was a light. Fletcher came to the door yawning and rubbing his eyes. He'd pulled on pants over his long johns and he was barefoot. He held the lamp high and blinked at me. "Boy," he grumbled, "what're you doin' out this time of night? Don't you know it's long past time all decent folks was in bed and rogues was on the road? Besides, this's Christmas eve. You ought'a be home. Well, come in, come in."

I stepped into the big barren living room and said, "I'm sorry to wake you, Mr. Fletcher, but I need some whiskey right away."

"Whiskey?" he scowled at me. "You're startin' pretty young, ain't you?"

"I need it for Lucifer. He's sick. He can't get up. Ma wants it to give him a—a boost."

He shuffled toward the kitchen and I followed. "Lucifer," he shook his head at the name. "That the pony Frank got from me?"

"Yes," I said.

"Sick you say? What's wrong with him?"

"I had to ride into town during the blizzard. He got frosted lung."

"That's bad," he muttered. "Real bad."

Two bottles stood on the counter in the kitchen. Both were empty. "Sorry," he said, "seems like I can't help you."

"What about some of your hands? Would they have some?"

"Could be. That just could be. That's good thinkin', Boy. Wait'll I get my boots on we'll go see."

He was maddeningly slow pulling on his boots, getting

into an old jacket, and lighting the lantern. He talked all the time. "Seen you ridin' that black devil, didn't I? Never thought anybody'd do that, let alone a saplin' like you. Just shows you can't never tell about a man or horse."

"Mr. Fletcher, can you hurry a little?" I said. "They're waiting for me."

"Relax, Boy," he said easily. "Horses been known to live for days with frosted lung. That's the trouble with young fellers these days. Can't never wait. Always in a hurry. Gotta rush here. Gotta rush there. Don't know what they're gonna do when they get there. Can't never take their time. All right, I'm ready."

When the lantern lit the interior of the bunkhouse, heads popped up from every bunk. "Hey, Sam, for the luva Mike. It ain't mornin' yet," someone grumbled.

"Boy needs whiskey for a sick horse," Fletcher said. "Any here?" A half-dozen bottles stood on a table. Some had liquor in them. Fletcher began pouring the liquor into one bottle. A voice complained, "You can't mix 'em, Sam."

"What's taste to a horse." Fletcher handed me a bottle more than three-quarters full of about four different brands. "Here you are, Boy. I hope it helps."

Going home, I gave Nellie the roughest run she'd ever had. When I walked into the barn they were putting a new hot blanket around Lucifer's chest. He still lay stretched out flat. I asked, "How is he?"

"About the same, I guess," Ma said. "We've got to get him up somehow. You did find a bottle."

"No, I went to Fletcher's for this."

"Well, bless his heart," Ma took the bottle. "Help Frank put the blanket on." She headed for the house.

We'd just nicely got it fastened in place and the sacks packed around when Ma returned. She had a different bottle with some kind of dark mixture. Frank asked, "What's that?"

"Whiskey and mighty strong coffee."

"Coffee?"

"Coffee's a stimulant, too." Ma sat down in the straw and cradled Lucifer's head in her lap. Frank tipped his head up and Ma worked the neck of the bottle into the corner of his mouth and tilted it. He didn't swallow. The liquid ran out. She stroked his neck, talked to him in a low intimate voice, and tried again. This time I saw the convulsive movement of muscles as he swallowed.

"Ah-h-h! that's it! That's it!" Frank's voice was jubilant. "He's taking it!"

I'll never forget that picture of Ma sitting there in the straw on the barn floor, the lantern glow making shining highlights in her black hair as she bent over Lucifer crooning softly. She coaxed him into swallowing the whole bottle of coffee-whiskey mixture.

Then she stood up. "Now then," she said very business-like, "we'll let him be. We'll keep on with the hot packs for a couple more hours. Then we'll give him some more coffee and whiskey and see what happens."

"You think he might get up then?" I asked hopefully.

"Christopher," Ma said soberly, "he'd better."

I went back to keeping the fire going and the hot water coming. Ma and Frank did all the wringing out of the blanket and packing it around Lucifer's chest.

I was about dead on my feet. Once Frank had to wake me to bring more water. I knew Ma was about at the end of her rope, too. There were strain lines around her mouth and a tired droop to her shoulders. Frank tried to get her to go up to the house and rest but she shook her head. "I've come this far," she said stubbornly, "I'm going to see it through."

Ellie slept the night without waking once.

Gray light was seeping into the barn and Frank had turned off the lantern when Ma decided to give Lucifer the next bottle of coffee and whiskey. As before she sat with his head in her lap and worked the neck of the bottle into a corner of his mouth and tipped it up. Frank and I watched anxiously.

Lucifer began to swallow almost immediately. He took the whole bottle without stopping.

"That's more like it," Frank said.

Ma patted Lucifer's head and stood up. If she'd been tired before she didn't show it now. "Now then, let's take the blanket off and try to get him up. Christopher, you get at his head. Frank, you take the rear. We'll try to heave him up like we did before. He's going to need all the help we can give him to make it."

We took the sacks off his legs and pushed him over to a lying down position. It seemed to me he helped a little, but maybe it was wishful thinking. Then I got hold of the halter on either side of his head, Frank had his tail and at Ma's nod we started pulling and lifting and coaxing him with our voices. He didn't seem to help at all and we accomplished nothing. Then Ma grabbed a whip off the wall and cut him sharply across the back and yelled at him. Startled, be began to scramble. Frank and I pulled and lifted harder than ever. Ma cut him again. The next instant with an almost human groan he heaved to his feet.

He stood legs braced, head down, trembling. For an instant I thought he was going to fall. Then his head slowly came up, his ears pricked forward. He turned his head and blew his breath in my face.

Ma said, "Lead him around a little."

I tugged gently on the halter. He took a step, then another. Very slowly, carefully, I led him around the small circle several times. Then Ma held a carrot under his nose. This time he took it and his big teeth crunched down.

Ma patted him and there were tears in her eyes. I realized something. You can't dislike an animal or a person after you've fought to save his life.

"He's going to be all right now, isn't he? He's going to get well?" I asked.

"He's going to be fine. It may take a couple of weeks before he's himself again."

"This was a big night's work," Frank said.

Ma leaned against the stall and pushed the hair wearily from her face. "I'm so tired."

Frank put an arm around her. "Come up to the house. I'm going to get the breakfast. Then you're going to bed."

I watched them walk toward the house arm in arm. The sun burst over Christmas Ridge and poured the day's first bright light into the valley. Ellie was almost well again. Lucifer was going to be all right. I had the .22 rifle I'd wanted. All I needed was the sight of those two people disappearing into the house together. This morning we'd become a family. It was the most wonderful Christmas Day I've ever known. I was so happy I actually hurt.